Law of
LOVE

First Edition.

ISBN: 978-1-915251-04-6

Cover design: © The Pretty Little Design Co.

Developmental Editing by Sara-Jane Higgins (Kat's Literary Services)

Editing by Kat Wyeth (Kat's Literary Services)

Proofreading by Louise Murphy (Kat's Literary Services)

Law of LOVE

K. LOWRIE

To having a crush and hoping for the best,

Author's Note

Law of Love is the first book in a new series, Lanes of Love, and introduces the Winters family.
This series will explore multiple tropes, and this book contains one of my favourite tropes:
Best Friend's Brother

CW: Mentions of parental abuse, drug use, murder and organised crime.

P.S. Law of Love is written in British English

Enjoy!

madison

PROLOGUE

THE SHOUTING ROSE, AND I CLAMPED MY HANDS over my ears and pressed my knees closer to my chest.

Mum and Dad were fighting again, the way they always did. I couldn't remember a time when my parents weren't arguing. They hated each other, but then they'd talk about how much they loved each other. That they were all they needed.

I didn't understand love.

'La-la-la.' Maybe if I was loud enough, I could drown them out.

I continued, repeating 'la-la-la', trying to cover their voices in my head.

It had never worked before, but maybe there was a first time for everything.

The dark of the wardrobe in my bedroom helped a little to block out my parents, but not seeing didn't change the horrible feeling in my belly. Didn't change what my ears heard.

Hiding in my wardrobe to block out the world had been

my coping mechanism for so long now, I didn't know how else to deal with it without exploding. I understood it only made me look more childish in the eyes of my parents, being thirteen and all.

More shouting. Mum crying.

'La-la-la!' My voice got louder. They would never hear me, though. Even if they did, they'd turn their anger towards me. It would unite them. Sometimes, having them angry at me was better than them being angry at each other.

A thud.

A shout.

A scream.

It took everything in me not to call out to my mum. They didn't like it when I got involved. It never ended well for me when I did.

'LA-LA-LA!'

I needed to leave. I couldn't sit and listen to it anymore.

My eyes burned with tears. My ears hurt from the force of my hands covering them, pressing them so hard they'd disappear inside my skull if I didn't stop.

What could I do?

The warmth and happiness of the Winters' home flashed through my head. They were always smiling there. Never shouting. Never so mad that their face turned the colour of a tomato, scrunched up with anger. They'd acted as my refuge more times than I could count.

Being around them, I understood a little bit about what it was to love.

My hands still clamped over my ears to block out the sound, I stood. I had to uncover my ears to grab my coat from its hanger, put it on, and open the door, but I did it as fast as I could.

Thud.

Slap.

Another scream, even louder than before.

The neighbours could hear, how could they not? But they'd never done anything to help me. To stop him. To stop her.

On quiet feet, I tiptoed down the hallway, passing the room my parents were in, and to the front door.

Neither of them heard me. They rarely did.

All they cared about was each other, for good and for bad.

Once I made it safely out the front door, I flew down the metal staircase inside our flat building to the door that led to the outside world. To the small glimpse of freedom I had in life.

The moment my bare feet hit the pavement, I ran fast to the Winters' house, not stopping for anything.

A route I used often.

Every day, after school, I went to my best friend's house for as long as I could, and afterwards, her parents drove me home.

My parents didn't even message to ask me where I went or spent my evenings. Half the time, I doubted they even noticed I was gone.

My best friend, Dottie Winters, had the best home and the *best* family. One I wished every time I blew out my birthday candles to be a part of for real, and not as an honorary member.

The house came into view, and I sped up, rushing to the door and banging on it with all my strength.

Tears blinded me, and when the door opened, the sobs I'd held in came pouring out.

'I'm s-so s-sorry for barging in like this.' I could barely control the wobble in my bottom lip.

'Madison,' a boy's voice said, and I blinked, focusing for the first time since landing on their doorstep. The person who opened the door wasn't Bonnie Winters, as expected. Nope. Instead, Dottie's oldest brother, Dylan, stood there with a scared look on his face. 'What's happened?'

My tongue froze. My entire body froze.

Dylan continued as if I wasn't statue-still and silent. He whispered, 'Your parents?'

I nodded—it was the most I could do—and wiped the tears from underneath my eyes. It was an unspoken thing, the truth about my parents, but the Winters knew without my saying much.

They never forced me to talk, and I loved them even more for it.

'It's okay.' He reached out and rubbed my arm. 'You're okay.'

The words settled, an ooey gooey sensation washing through me at the kindness in his eyes. Truly seeing him for the very first time.

'Thank you.'

'Come on,' he said, reaching out a hand to me, urging me to take it. 'Let's get inside and find Dot. I'll even let the two of you chill in my room if you want?'

Dylan's room had the coolest set-up. Long comfy bean bag chairs lived in the corner, with a large TV and multiple gaming consoles in front of them. It was a rare occurrence to be allowed inside. He considered it his sanctuary, and even though he lived away at uni now and we could probably enter whenever we wanted, we all still thought of it as his.

Tears filled my eyes again at the sympathy shining in his. 'Yes, please.'

'No more tears,' he said, his voice gentle. 'You're home now.'

It was the most perfect thing to say, coming from the most perfect lips I'd ever seen.

Dylan's warm and inviting smile gave way to butterflies in my tummy.

How comes I'd never noticed how beautiful he was before?

'Thank you,' I said, taking his hand. A spark of electricity travelled from his skin to mine.

Wow.

It was official.

I had a huge crush on my best friend's older brother.

madison

THICK, WHITE, SUGARY—AND EXTREMELY STICKY—icing stuck to every strand of my blonde curled hair, and I wanted to cringe. Shy away from everybody around me.

But I couldn't do that.

Not with every eye in the place fixated on me.

And not just every eye of every person at the party, but also the eyes of all those watching along at home or on the go via the livestream. Social media ensured people would know my embarrassment from far and wide, with no way to hide from it.

Sometimes, being an influencer sucked.

'Happy birthday, Dottie!' I shrieked alongside everybody else, my mouth wide, my smile constant. It was my best friend's eighteenth birthday party, after all, and I had to look the part at all times. My followers expected it from me, and I never wanted to disappoint them. Even if I currently had icing in my hair, kindly put there by Dottie's current "boyfriend" as a "joke".

Dottie, looking absolutely stunning, sans icing in her

styled hair, wearing a gorgeous black dress covered in sparkles, stood beaming beside her cake, a genuine look of happiness blinding everyone around her.

'Thank you all for coming to my party! I love and appreciate every single one of you for taking the time out of your busy schedules to come and celebrate little ol' me.' She giggled, and it took a lot for me to hold my eye roll in. Knowing her as well as I did, I highly doubted she loved and appreciated every single person here. Some of them she'd met in the toilets of a bar last week at some event or other and had invited them simply for the exposure they'd give her on their social media accounts.

A lot of what people watched online was fake, and false, and a shiny lie. Yet we were the vultures who used it to our advantage.

Brushing her dark locks from her face, she continued, 'The first eighteen years have been wonderful, and I know that year nineteen is going to be my best yet! Thank you again, and enjoy the party.'

Dottie took a step to move away from the front of the stage, ready to enjoy the rest of her evening, but she paused.

'None of this would've been possible without my best friend, Madison.'

Ah, I was an afterthought, as usual.

She turned to face me, reaching her arm out to pull me closer.

I went willingly. Or as willingly as I could in front of a crowd without looking like I didn't want her to touch me. Unexpected or unnecessary touch irritated me, and Dottie knew it, yet she crossed the boundary anyway. Maybe because I'd never actually set it as one with her.

The cameras pointed at us made sure that I remained natural and smiling. Dottie's grip was tight on my forearm, her unsaid words penetrating my brain with every bruise she left: *do not mess this up for us.*

'Mads here arranged everything, and I don't know where my life would be without her. Madison, you're truly the best.'

My cheeks warmed. Dottie meant every word, and it didn't sit well in my gut that I hated every second of being here. It made me feel like a bad person for not enjoying the same things as her.

The two of us had stumbled into our jobs as beauty and lifestyle influencers, and now we were established and making good money, no way out had revealed itself to me.

It had begun simply enough. Something fun to pass the time.

It all started when the two of us posted on our socials what we were doing each day. The outfits we wore to college. That kind of thing. Typical day-to-day girl stuff.

After that, our following grew, basically overnight.

We went to a Dagger concert—only the coolest rock band to exist FYI—and a clip we posted of the two of us dancing with the guitarist, Banks, in the background went viral, like millions of views viral, and our presence catapulted.

Now neither of us could do anything without it being documented.

If we went shopping, we posted our purchases on our stories. If we went to the cinema, we posted a video review clip the moment we left the screen. If we did or said anything, there were thousands of people viewing and liking and sharing whatever it was, and there was no moment these days where we weren't switched on.

Thankfully, the crowd around Dottie's cake dissipated, and the party resumed as if there'd been no interruption at all. Dottie's hand still grasped my arm, but she'd released her hold a smidge. Maybe the bruising wouldn't be too bad. Luckily for me, my make-up skills could cover a bruise in no time. A skill I'd employed more often than I should have.

'You having fun?' Dottie asked, and I nodded, unsure of what else to say. I may not have been having fun, but I also wasn't totally miserable either. I hated lying to her, yet with so many people around, I couldn't be honest. Not at her party with the night still young.

And I hoped the night wouldn't be all bad.

Why, you ask? Well, because Madison's oldest brother, Dylan, would arrive soon.

Here's the part where I tell you I *still* have the biggest crush on him and have done for a really, really, *really* long time. Never waning, never disappearing. Simply there, a fact known only to myself.

Dylan was gorgeous. All tanned and tall and everything I thought and fantasised about.

The downside to my delusion? He was thirty, a big hot-shot lawyer in the city, and he didn't know I existed.

Okay, so maybe a slight exaggeration.

Of course he knew I existed. Dottie and I became best friends way back in the day, and I'd spent a lot of summers, and many an evening, at their house, playing with the rest of the Winters siblings. Dylan was a lot older than us, though, which meant he'd been off doing cool things with his friends while we stayed home and played with dolls.

Another cool thing about being an included member of the Winters clan was that I got to take part in their monthly bowling tournaments. I rarely missed one, in the hopes I'd get a glimpse of him, but for the last few years, Dylan had missed every single one.

To Dylan, I expected that he saw me as his annoying kid sister's annoying friend, and I doubted anything I did would change that, even if I wanted to.

And I *wanted* to, more than anything.

Dottie's harsh whisper once we were at the back of the stage dragged me away from my thoughts. 'Nathan's here. Did you know?' She pointed discreetly into the crowd, and I pressed onto my tiptoes to see where she pointed. Nathan was her ex-boyfriend, the supposed one who got away, even though we were still teenagers and had barely lived our lives yet. Something Dottie ignored whenever I told her.

'I'm happy to live in my delusions, Madison.'

I shook my head. 'Can't see him.'

'Wonder if he has his girlfriend with him?'

'I'd assume so,' I murmured. 'They're pretty much joined at the hip these days ever since they went off to university together. I'm surprised they came.'

'Me too. Maybe it means—'

I cut her off before she could go on some kind of hopeful tangent. 'It means nothing, Dottie. Who wouldn't want to get in on a free bar in town? That's all.'

'You're so negative, Mads. You always think the worst of people.'

'No,' I emphasised. 'I'm a realist, and I think of people exactly what they put out into the universe. If somebody acts like a toad and croaks like a toad, chances are, they're a stinking toad.'

'Oh, hush.' Dottie laughed, rubbing her hand on my arm more gently, soothing my blooming bruise. 'We'll make an optimist of you yet.'

'Dot, I *am* an optimist.' I laughed. 'I'm also a realist and know when people aren't worth your time.'

She laughed harder. 'Yes, but you can let me dream.'

'Well, it's your funeral.' The two of us made our way to the edge of the stage, ready to descend the steps back into the madness that was a night at Muse.

My eyes darted around the vast room, and even though I told myself it wasn't to search for Dylan, I could be honest and admit—to myself, at least—it was one hundred per cent to search for Dylan. Usually, you could spot him from a mile away as he literally stood head and shoulders above everybody else, but neither his head nor his shoulders were anywhere in sight.

I couldn't stay quiet any longer. 'Dots, have you seen—'

The end of my sentence cut off and floated in the atmosphere as my feet were taken out from underneath my body, stumbled down the stage steps, and for a millisecond, floated in mid-air.

CHAPTER 2

dylan

RUNNING LATE USED TO PISS ME OFF, A REAL IRK OF mine, but recently, me running late happened more and more often.

Work consumed me.

The case consumed me.

To the point where I forgot the time, forgot the day, forgot every and all of my responsibilities.

Like attending my baby sister's eighteenth birthday party.

Shit, shit, shit.

My legs weren't getting me to my destination fast enough, and clearly, I was talking aloud too because people looked at me with a raised brow and a concerned scowl.

Ever since she'd become an influencer, my youngest sister, Dottie, lived for the attention of having her every move documented and watched by thousands. She'd always loved being the centre of everything, and the influencer crap she did these days only helped to fuel it further.

The club came into view, and I ran the last few paces,

almost knocking the bouncer down with my shout: 'Dylan Winters!'

The amused bouncer nodded and raised the rope for me to pass through.

Thank fuck for that.

Inside, the music thumped too loud, and I cringed at the writhing people dressed to impress. I'd lost track of time, so I still wore my suit from work. It wouldn't have been worth stopping at home first, as the lack of me being there already annoyed Dottie. I didn't have to physically be in her presence to know that.

The last five texts from her told me as much.

Dottie
Dylan, where are you?

Are you here yet?

Are you close?

Have you forgotten?!

DYLAN!

One of my other sisters, Dahlia, appeared on my right with a frown. Dahlia was two years younger than me but acted older. The two of us were close. Close enough to live together, even.

'Dylan, where have you been? They've already sung Happy Birthday and done the cake.'

'Lost track of time.'

She rolled her eyes. 'Of course you did. This case is taking over your life. You ever gonna tell me about it?'

'You know I can't do that.' I shook my head, annoyed she'd asked me again when I'd made it clear I couldn't say anything about it to her—or anybody, for that matter. 'Where's Dottie now?'

'Still on the stage wi—'

I didn't wait for her to finish her sentence.

Located at the back was the relatively small stage at Muse, barely big enough for a crowd of ten people at most, and when I craned my neck, I could just about make out Dottie in the crush.

My elbows barged people out of the way, and I threw a quick wave in my parents' direction, spotting them over by the bar. I'd head there once I'd said happy birthday. God forbid I choose to stop and talk to other people before my little sister.

What happened next came in a flash.

One moment, I was waving at my parents, head turned in their direction, foot raised to ascend the steps.

The next, somebody sprawled on the floor at my feet, having landed with an almighty thud.

The seconds in between? Well, they were lost to me.

Not lost to the many cameras pointed in our direction, though.

No doubt my foolish manoeuvre was finding its way onto the interweb right that second because, of course, a minimum of ten people had caught it on camera.

'You're such an oaf, Dylan!' Dottie narrowed her gaze on me. 'You could've taken Madison's eye out.'

I looked around but couldn't spot Madison anywhere.

Only the poor influencer on the floor struggling to get to her feet. Best help the creature before my actions were blasted online as being ungentlemanly.

Dottie would never forgive me for bringing shame her way.

'I am so sorry about that,' I said, reaching down to the girl. 'Let me help you.'

Damn. The *creature* on the floor, now standing before me, was Madison Jones, looking ... absolutely bloody perfect.

In the years since I'd seen her in person last, she'd blossomed into something I couldn't quite describe. Every part of me awakened looking at her, and my heart sank when I realised just who I stood ogling.

My youngest sister's best friend.

In other words: a girl completely out of bounds.

'I'm sorry, Madison,' I said, my voice gruff. 'I wish I could tell you what happened in a way that makes sense, but it's like my brain's already erased it.'

Madison brushed her blonde curled—yet sticky?—hair behind her ears, a brittle smile on her face. 'It's fine.' Then, like a dimmer switch turning the bulb to the brightest setting, her entire demeanour changed to air and light. The transformation only made my heart beat faster. 'It's all good, Dylan. Not like you'd ever hurt me on purpose.' She laughed.

Hurt her? The words settled in the fog of my brain.

'Shit, are you hurt? Do you need anything? Can I do anything?' My mouth moved at the speed of light, barely leaving space for her to get a word in.

Huh, suppose Dottie could sometimes be right. I was an oaf.

She brushed me and the dirt from her dress off. 'I'm fine, promise.' She turned her beaming megawatt smile to the watching crowd and giggled. 'What am I like?'

I didn't want to look at her funny or anything, but jeez, everything was a performance with these two, wasn't it?

I'd seen Dottie hide her true feelings enough; switch on the persona her followers expected to see.

'How about the three of us get away from the stage and stop making a spectacle of ourselves?' Dottie announced like the drill sergeant she was at heart. 'Come on, Mads. Dylan.'

Without waiting for us to agree or say anything at all, Dottie flounced down the steps and turned right, opening a door previously hidden by a curtain, beckoning us both to follow her.

In life, I found it a lot easier to do as she said, and clearly, Madison recognised that, too, as she followed with the same silent obedience as me.

THE ROOM DOTTIE sequestered us became even smaller once all three of us were inside.

My eyes wanted to take in the room, but with Dottie standing dead centre, her arms folded across her chest, feet tapping on the floor, waiting for something from me, she was all I could see.

Best get my apology over with and let the grovelling commence.

'Dot, I am so sorry for being so late.'

'Dylan,' she said, her tone one of reproach. 'Let me guess ...' She rubbed her bottom lip, ever the actress. 'Something came up at the office related to your *big case* and you lost track of time and *that's* why you're showing up at your little sister's *eighteenth* birthday party over three hours late?'

'I—'

She waved me off. 'Save it. At this point, it isn't me you should be saying sorry to.' She stopped tapping her foot and focused her attention on Madison. 'How's the face? The oaf do any permanent damage?'

'Oh, no. Honestly, it's not a big deal, Dot. Please don't make it one.' Madison touched her face, patting the soft skin underneath her right eye. I hated to see her in pain. It took me back to a time when she'd often arrive at our house covered in bruises or cuts. Even now, years later, you could still make out the small scar that ran through her bottom lip.

'But there's a bruise forming already!' Dottie loved hysterics. She grazed her fingers against Madison's face, turning her to inspect every angle. 'Good thing you're a whizz with make-up. Am I right?'

The two of them laughed, only one of which sounded genuine.

'I'm sorry, Madison.' My eyes were fixed on the area of her face, turning a dark shade of pink, growing darker with each second. 'Somebody knocked me, and ...' I shook my head. 'There's no excuse.'

Madison turned to look me in the eye, a blush on her cheeks. 'Honestly, stop apologising. We're good. And your sister's right, I can totally cover this.' She shrugged. 'Not like you did it on purpose, and don't worry, the footage making the rounds via the internet will show everybody how much of a perfect gentleman you are. Wouldn't be surprised if you got your own fans from this actually.'

Me and my whole family knew the two of them had a lot of followers, but being somebody who didn't use social media much, I wasn't sure *just* how many they'd accumulated.

I winced. 'How many people will watch it, do you think?'

'Oh, loads.' Dottie waved her hand as if the actual number was inconsequential, finally taking a step back from Madison.

'And loads equals ...'

'A few hundred thousand.' Dottie tossed her head, proud. 'Maybe more.'

'A few hundred thousand?' I repeated, my voice higher than normal. That number didn't even feel real to me. Like, how?

'Well, yeah.' Dottie answered the rhetorical question. 'Between us, we've got like 500k, and not to mention the people at the party have loads, too. Pretty sure one model I invited has over five million.'

'Five million?' I sputtered.

Dottie nodded, unaware of my inner turmoil.

I liked to stay low profile, and any time she'd asked me if she could post a picture of me, I said no. It had totally slipped my mind that the party would mean being online in one way or another—even if only in the background of an influencer's photo.

'Right.' I nodded my head back. 'Well, okay, then. Happy birthday, Dots.'

My sister came into my outstretched arms without a fight, accepting my hug and the kiss on her head with ease.

Even though I didn't want to face Madison again, worried she or Dottie would notice my reaction to her, I couldn't help myself. I needed another look at her, not to mention I needed to apologise again, even though she'd told me not to.

'I'm sorry again, Madison,' I said, letting go of Dottie and turning to where Madison had stood.

But only empty space remained.

dylan

TAYLOR & ROBERTS, THE PLACE I'D WORKED AT ever since leaving university, acted as a social hub on a Monday morning.

The start of the work week always had people refreshed and ready to gossip before the slog of law took over.

With a swagger in my step, I pushed the double glass doors open and faced Dawn with a wide smile.

Dawn had been the receptionist for longer than even she could remember. She acted as a mother figure to all of us, and even though we told her on the daily to retire, she had no intention of doing such a thing.

'Morning, Dawn.' My arms rested on the top of the counter. 'How was your weekend?'

'Dylan.' She smiled, her gums showing. 'Oh, it was wonderful! The grandchildren all stayed over, and I was in my element. It's so lovely to have all five of them under my roof at the same time. Not sure my Jerry would agree with that mind. They rather disrupt his TV watching.'

I laughed, the image of her husband, Jerry, disgruntled,

trying to watch football in my head. Jerry was no-nonsense, and I'd always wondered how the two of them gelled together.

'Glad you had a good one. Half term soon, isn't it? You all heading to the house in Spain?'

She nodded, her excitement making me excited, and I wasn't the one going to lounge around in the sun. Couldn't even remember the last time I'd done something like that. 'I'm through the roof about it. It may not be Disney, but it's a close second!'

'I'm sure it is.' I pushed myself up and away from the counter. 'Best be off to make some coffee now, otherwise, Noah won't be happy.'

'You run along now, dear. Say hello to Noah for me! He slipped past before I got here.'

'Will do.'

If Dawn hadn't started when Noah arrived, it meant he'd been here at the crack of dawn. He lived in the city so didn't have the hour commute from Lakeland the way I did, so he spent more hours in the office than me—and that was a lot of bloody hours.

Three other employees were milling around the drinks station, and I said a quick hello.

It wouldn't do to get caught up in their conversation. Knowing them, they'd be at it for hours before finally getting some work done.

Not everybody at the firm worked as hard as me and Noah, but our bosses, Mick Taylor and Jeoffrey Roberts, treated everybody the same. Sometimes it pissed me off, but I'd never say anything to them about it.

I'd learned since starting at the firm, it was easier to put your head down and do the work. They respected that most.

While I waited for the machine to be free, I grabbed my phone from my pocket and pulled up social media—again. Ever since Dottie's party, I looked every hour. At first, I told myself it was so I knew what was out there regarding me knocking poor Madison down the stage steps. To watch the video of my humiliation taken from at least ten different angles.

But there were only so many times I could look at that.

So then I'd gone to Madison's profile and had a nose. Just to see what she'd been up to since I spoke to and saw her last. To get a feel for her life.

I ended up scrolling through to the start of her feed, liking posts as I went.

It was stupid of me, but once I liked a post from a year ago? Well, I had to continue.

Her bright smile lit me up inside, her most recent picture—one of her and Dottie at the local café owned by my parents' friends.

I double tapped.

'The machine's free,' an intern said to me, a too-wide smile on her face.

'Oh, thanks.' I put my phone away and sorted the coffees, ready to start my day.

With two Americanos in hand, I headed to Noah's office.

***

THE DOOR OPENED as I reached it.

Mick and Jeoffrey exited the room, smiling when they spotted me standing there holding the two steaming mugs of coffee.

Mick nodded. 'Morning, Dylan.'

'Morning,' I said, returning the nod. It was such a guy thing to do, but the nod was catching. If thrown your way, you had no choice but to return it. 'Fine day, isn't it?'

'Very.' Jeoffrey clapped his hands together. 'Noah will fill you in on this week's focus.'

'Can't wait.' The phrase sounded sarcastic, but really, work thrilled me. Gave me a buzz. And any new information could only make our jobs easier—not that we'd had any as of late. Things were ... slow, to put it mildly.

Mick and Jeoffrey moved on, greeting anyone they passed. Partners of a company happy to greet their employees? They're a rare breed indeed.

'Those two are lively this morning,' I said, taking a step into Noah's office. 'Suppose they're on a cloud right now, ay?'

Noah laughed. 'Suppose they are.'

If I had to state my best friend, something I wouldn't do unless asked under duress, Noah would be who I'd name.

The two of us met at university, and once we'd gained our law degrees, we both applied to intern at Taylor & Roberts together. We'd been co-workers and gym buddies ever since.

I handed him his coffee. 'I suppose I should congratulate you on making partner.'

Noah smiled, shaking his head. 'Still can't believe it's happened to tell you the truth.'

'What did Hallie have to say about it?'

Hallie was Noah's new girlfriend. Me and my sister, Dahlia, set the two of them up on a blind date, and lucky for us, it worked out for the best, otherwise, we'd never have heard the end of it.

'She's thrilled, naturally.' His smile widened. 'Although she told me that if I missed too many special occasions because I was working, she may feel differently.'

'Understandable. Dottie nearly killed me Saturday night when I finally showed.'

'Yes, but Dottie is a monster when she thinks she's being overlooked.'

I couldn't even defend my sister because he spoke the truth.

'Alright,' I said, sitting down in the chair opposite his desk, waiting for him to do the same before I continued. 'Tell me this week's focus.'

Noah rubbed his stubbled jaw. 'You're not gonna like it.'

I stayed silent. There wasn't much regarding our case against The Syndicate I liked as of late, and I doubted his words would change that.

'We've got nothing new. Informants are drying up, and without the ever-elusive hard drive, we've got shit.'

'But the hard drive's only a rumour,' I said. 'We can't waste our time on it. Not until it materialises.'

'And what if it never does? Those who spoke to the police believe Jaws's daughter stole it twenty-eight years ago, and it's never been seen since.'

'His daughter is protected. Nobody knows where she is. Or who she is. She's a dead end.'

'I know.' Noah's face was grim. 'Which is why we're no further than we were three bloody years ago.'

'That's not true. We've made progress.'

'Not enough. The police are about to pull the plug on the whole thing. Take down those they can and leave it for a while. Wait for something big before starting again.'

'But that's ridiculous. The Syndicate needs to pay for what they've done.'

'Of course I agree, but nothing's that simple, and our hands are tied if the police withdraw the funding.'

The Syndicate, a large crime organisation in the city, had existed for years, ruling in the shadows, but three years ago, the second-in-command, Lawrence Knight, slipped up. The police had asked our firm to collect the data and use the information they found to build a case so that one day, they could finally bring it all down.

'But we've got a fuck ton of evidence!' My hands gripped my hair, frustration pouring off me in waves. My entire career hinged on the outcome of the case. Fuck, I'd lost a relationship because of this case. It couldn't all have been for nothing. I wouldn't allow it.

Noah sighed. 'Even with all the evidence we have, it still isn't enough.'

'Well, we can't give up.' My words sounded stronger than the belief I had in them. 'Something will give. It has to.'

Noah laughed. 'Here's hoping one day soon a nice dead body lands in our laps, a witness to boot, and then maybe, just maybe, it'll be the downfall of them all.'

madison

'Dot, are you sure you want to move in with Dylan and Dahlia?' I finished taping the packing box, making sure the tape lay flat on the corners, and rested back on my heels, inspecting my work. I'd impressed myself actually.

We'd been packing up Dottie's childhood bedroom for hours and were yet to make much progress.

The room was filled with destruction.

Teddy bears were strewn all over the floor, pillows and blankets upended by tornado Dottie.

Dot stopped packing the box in front of her, if we could call placing two items inside as packing, and sat back on her haunches, mimicking me. 'You think it's a bad idea?'

'Not a bad idea as such.' I shrugged. 'Guess I don't get why you wouldn't want a place of your own.'

She looked at me like I was missing the point entirely, which, clearly, I was.

'But Dill and Lia have an empty third bedroom. The

two of them are always so busy with work that they're never there anyway. It'll basically be like living on my own.' She went back to slowly placing items in the box. 'Plus, they're giving me a deal on rent so I can save up for a place of my own.'

Once again, the generosity within the Winters family set something off in my stomach.

My whole life, they'd shown how generous they were, and I'd be forever grateful for them. It may have started with my friendship with Dottie, but since then, every single person in the Winters family has shown me love.

It made sense Dylan was rarely home, being a big hot-shot lawyer in the city an hour away. Dahlia, the second Winters sibling, co-owned a salon with her best friend and spent long hours making the town of Lakeland look their best.

'As long as you're sure,' I said, returning to my task.

'I am. As much as I like living here,' she gestured around the pink-walled room, 'I need my freedom. Mum and Dad are great and all, but I'll love them more if there's distance between us. Dad always needs to know where I am at all times, and we both know Mum can be quite overbearing.'

Bonnie, her mum, could be quite overbearing, but at least it came from a place of love. It wasn't worth pointing it out to Dottie, though. She'd only wave it away, an unimportant fact of life.

I'd give anything to have a mum who loved me enough to *be* overbearing.

I laughed. 'Plus, if you're home with no plans, they're much more likely to rope you into helping out at the lanes.'

'Right!' Dottie nodded her head with enthusiasm. 'And

don't get me wrong, I love the alley. I just don't want to spend every moment of my free time there.'

Dottie's parents owned Lakeland Lanes, the local bowling alley, and had done our whole lives. Purchasing it was the reason they originally moved to town when Dylan was two years old. A story they told often, with much fondness.

When Dottie and I were younger, we loved hanging out at the lanes with our friends, playing as many games as we wanted for free. I'm surprised they managed to stay in business with the amount they let us get away with.

On the last Sunday of every month, the Winters held a family bowling tournament, and I joined them most months when I didn't have an event to attend.

Just another example of them taking me under their wing.

'Did you interact any more with Nathan on Saturday?' I asked, changing the subject back to something Dottie loved to talk about—her own life.

A week had passed since her party, and we'd not had time to debrief since. After I left her and Dylan in that closet room, I'd stuck to the shadows, leaving not long afterwards.

'No.' She sucked her teeth. 'He and his girlfriend were packing on the PDA the whole night.'

'Ew.'

'Yep.' Dottie sat back again, even though I'd only seen her add two more items to the box in front of her, and she brushed her hair behind her ear. 'Clearly, he wanted me to know about them. One day soon, he'll realise we're supposed to be together.'

'But you're dating what's-his-name? The model guy?'

Or at least I thought he was a model. Dottie dated in a way that was as erratic as her, dating someone new with each passing week. 'Drake, or Drew, or Drey, or something?'

'*Braydon.*' An eye twitched. 'We're not serious or anything. I'm not sure I even like him that much.'

'And you couldn't have figured that out *before* he covered me in icing and cake?'

The two of us continued packing in peace.

So many items were ones I recognised from over the years: the blanket her sister, Dana, had knitted for her when she went through her knitting and crochet phase; the dress Dottie had worn on her sixteenth birthday; the first pair of shoes she received, gifted by a big designer name.

'Oh em gee, do you remember these?' Dottie thrust two items in my face. 'Gosh, we loved these so much!'

She placed them in my hand, and my heart melted at the sight of our Pocket Pals. They were all the rage when we were younger. A gadget with a screen that we had to feed, put to sleep, and play with.

'We pressured your mum into keeping them alive for us while we were at school,' I said.

I placed them down with care. These were artefacts from Mads and Dottie past, after all.

'And my dad would watch them while we bowled, yet he never fed them. Pretty sure yours died because of his negligence.'

Dottie tried to turn them on, but the screens remained blank, before throwing them into her box. So much for care.

'Let's be thankful he was nowhere near as negligent in his real parenting.'

The two of us chuckled, the memories of the room and the items within it overtaking us.

'On the subject of parents,' Dottie said, and my stomach sank. I wanted to stop her but didn't know how. 'Have you heard from your mum? I know last time I asked she hadn't tried to contact you but ...'

'Nope.' I smiled. It was false. 'Not since the day I moved out.'

'That's good then.'

I nodded. It was better than good, but I didn't trust it. Not yet. My mum was a vulture, and the moment she found out about my job, she'd show her face when I least expected it.

'What time are Dylan and Dahlia expecting us?' I checked my smartwatch. Already a quarter to three, and we were no closer to achieving our task than when we started.

'I said we'd head over there around five at the latest.' Dottie checked the time on her own watch and winced. 'Maybe I should message them and say we're running late.'

I coughed.

'That *I'm* running late,' she amended.

I waved her off. 'Pretty sure they'll know already. You're rarely on time.'

'Right.' She laughed. 'It doesn't matter anyway. For once in his life, Dylan doesn't have plans and is home all day, so he'll be there to help whenever we show up.'

'Oh.'

The sound left me before I could keep it in. I'd got it in my head that Dahlia waited at the house for us, and that Dylan would be gone.

Not that I didn't want to be around Dylan because I did. I always wanted to be around Dylan. But I didn't want to act like a fool around him.

Seeing him on Saturday for the first time in at least a year only made my crush on him burn brighter. It had fanned the flames of a childhood crush into something a little more adult. Not to mention I'd seen him liking my posts and viewing every story I put up in the week since. Hard not to look into it as more than him being nice. *Wishful thinking.*

It wouldn't be smart to tempt fate by putting myself into a position where I could end up drooling merely from looking at him.

Dylan was my best friend's older brother and way out of my league.

He had that smart, sexy aura surrounding him that set my soul into another stratosphere, but I was more than aware he probably only viewed me as an annoying little sister who bugged him.

'Not a problem, is it?' Dottie's eyes wrinkled at the edges. 'I know he's been a moody bastard ever since Caroline cheated on him, but it makes sense. The poor guy thought he'd spend his life with her, and now he's living with his younger sisters and burying himself with boring work.'

'I don't think he's moody.' I brushed stray hairs away from my face. 'And you're right, it's totally justified if he is a little sour about it all. Caroline didn't deserve him.'

'I wish I could set him up with a nice girl, ya know? One who'd treat him well and be a part of the family. Someone you and I could add to our girls' days. Not that I need another sister—two plus you is more than enough, thanks— but it'd be good for him to be happy.'

'I think in his own way, he is happy. Yeah, you may find his work boring, but it's all he's ever wanted to do.'

Dottie's eyes assessed me. I felt as if she could see right through me.

'You're not interested in him, are you?'

Was my face burning up? 'N-no.'

Her eyes narrowed further. 'Well, good. And don't be getting any ideas either. He's off-limits, as you well know.' She laughed, bitter. 'You're the only one of my friends who's never tried to hook up with either of my brothers.'

I nodded. 'I'm just saying he'll find someone in his own time who'll be perfect for him,' I said.

'True.' Dottie rubbed at some packing tape stuck on the hem of her dress. 'I don't think I'll ever understand him.'

I nodded, absent-minded.

I'd be a monster if I didn't want Dylan to be happy, but I also wouldn't lie to myself and say it'd thrill me to know he was with another girl either.

Maybe I needed to grow some courage and ask him out. I'd noticed the way he looked at me on Saturday, and it wasn't *un*interested. Plus, the social stalking had to mean something, right?

Dottie, of course, could never know I entertained such thoughts.

What was the worst that could happen?

Oh, yeah. He could say no, and that'd make family engagements awkward for all eternity. Plus, I could lose Dottie as my best friend ...

But a niggle sat in the back of my brain. The one that kept me up at night. The one that convinced me to make stupid, impulsive decisions once every five years.

What if he said yes?
Only one way to find out for certain.

madison

BY THE TIME DOTTIE AND I ACTUALLY ARRIVED AT her new home, my resolve to even hint to Dylan about a date had disappeared almost entirely.

Dylan and Dahlia lived in an average detached two-storey home, with a neat red-brick driveway and a dark-red front door. The kind of home I'd dreamed of living in ever since I was a kid.

One car already sat on the driveway.

Dylan's.

My stomach swirled the way it always did when my nerves were about to get the better of me.

Big, deep breaths.

Dottie and I got out of her car, and the moment my foot touched the beautiful brick ground, the front door swung open to reveal a rather pissed-off-looking Dylan.

'What time do you call this?' he called across to us, his tone not quite angry but also not that happy either. 'You told me you were aiming for five. I've been waiting for you to grace me with your presence for hours.'

Dottie sighed, the weight of the world forever living on her dainty shoulders. 'You told me you didn't have plans today, Dill,' she pointed out, no room in her mind to even take in Dylan's complaint as anything real. 'I didn't think it'd be an issue.'

He brushed his hand through his hazelnut hair and huffed, exasperated at his youngest sister. 'Of course you wouldn't. You exist in Land Dot, and we're the side characters.'

Dottie opened the boot, ready to grab boxes, but paused and turned to look at Dylan. I still hovered by my door, afraid to shatter the fraught atmosphere further by closing the passenger side door.

'Dylan,' Dottie said, using his full name to disarm. 'Did you have plans today?'

'No,' he sputtered. 'But you could've at least messaged to say you were running super late! It's gone eight, Dottie.'

Dottie frowned at her brother, wrinkles forming in between her perfectly styled eyebrows, and I held in my laugh at her confusion.

You see, Dottie was the kind of person who sometimes forgot about other people. As far as I could tell, she never did it with malicious intent, and most of the time, she didn't even realise she did it. But she did it, nonetheless.

Dylan had got one thing right: she lived in Land Dot, waiting for us to be her sidekicks whenever the adventure called for us. In her head, it was her world, and we were all living in it for her amusement and happiness.

Dottie answered after a much longer pause than it should've been. 'Huh. Not gonna lie, but it didn't seem important.'

I laughed, unable to hold it in. It wouldn't do to point out that she had thought to send a message, and I was the one who waved it off. Clearly, our conversation had already made its way to the back recesses of her brain, never to see the light of day again.

I didn't want Dylan to be mad at me, but for once, I was just as much at fault as Dottie.

Dylan shook his head, frustration thick in the air, and rolled his eyes. Like me, her actions didn't surprise him in the slightest. We all let her get away with too much. 'No, I can imagine it didn't.'

'Hey, Dylan,' I said, opening my mouth knowing the moment had passed, finally getting to close the door I'd held on to for the past few minutes. 'Sorry we're so late. You know what Dot's like when focused on a task.'

'You mean distracted and slow?'

'Exactly like that.' I laughed. If anybody understood Dottie, it was her siblings. 'But she found her Barbie from when we were six, so the day was not lost.'

'The one that still has all its hair, or ...'

'Oh no.' I shook my head, the gravity of the words making my mood solemn. 'The one she cut all the hair from to prove a point to Dahlia that she could be a hairdresser, too.'

'Ah.' He dragged out the one syllable, his perfect brown eyes glinting as he smiled over at his little sister. 'That one.'

'Yes, yes,' Dottie said with a stamp of her foot. 'I'll have you know; I would've made a wonderful hairdresser had I not got into social media.'

Dylan continued to smile, all indulgent. 'Course you

would, Dots.' He assessed my face. 'You're looking a lot better than the last time I saw you.'

I touched the skin under my eye; the sting had faded after a week.

'Good thing Madison's eye's healed,' Dottie piped up. Dylan's head snapped in her direction, startled. 'People online had a field day with that one.'

My skin bristled.

'I'm sorry again,' Dylan said, and I shook my head.

'Nope, no more sorries.'

The three of us quietened, and I took it as my cue to move to the boot of the car and start unloading the boxes filled with crap Dottie insisted she couldn't bin.

'Let me do that, Madison,' Dylan said, his voice coming from a lot closer than expected. My body gave a little jolt at his proximity. Even his scent was alluring. 'I'm sure you've done the lion's share of the work today.'

I waved it off. 'It wasn't too bad. Kind of fun to find the toys we used to love when we were ten.'

'In my head, the two of you still are ten.' He chuckled, all warmth, yet my responding chuckle sounded so fake. With one sentence, he'd doused the fire burning away in the pit of my stomach and covered it with a fire-smothering blanket until barely a flicker remained. 'I forget you're both considered adults now.'

Considered adults? Jeez. He knew how to stab that knife in deep and twist it, my guts sputtering out onto the hard ground, flopping around for all to see.

'Ten was nearly half a life ago for Madison.' Dottie called from the front door, disrupting our conversation in a way only she could. 'Stop chit-chatting, you two. We've got a bedroom to fill with stuff!'

She swanned into the open doorway, apparently having decided we could handle the boxes without her help, and Dylan and I glanced at the overstuffed car.

'She's not exaggerating when she says a lot of stuff, is she?' Dylan leaned past me and grabbed the closest box, his warm, bare arm grazing against mine, causing chills to travel along my spine. I needed to put a dampener on my lust for him—and fast. 'I'm sorry about her.'

'You're not the one who should apologise.' I gestured in the direction Dottie had disappeared.

'We all spoiled her, what with her being the youngest and all.'

'You did.' Not like I would deny it. 'But it meant I got spoiled growing up too, and I can't be mad about that.'

Dylan handed me the box and paused, looking directly into my eyes. 'I was sorry to learn about your dad.'

Every fibre in my body seized. 'Don't be,' I muttered, stepping away from him, a box in my arms. The conversation topic was off-limits.

His eyes wrinkled at the corners, narrowing on me, but he said nothing more. The pity shining from them would've had me bolting if he were anyone else.

I needed a change of topic, pronto.

I walked to the front door, knowing he followed me, and soundlessly made my way up the stairs to the room Dottie would call hers.

I'd spent enough time there that I knew my way around.

'You'll never guess what we found earlier,' I said, placing the box down in the centre of the room.

Dylan did the same with his box and smiled at me. 'Is that an invitation to guess?'

'If you think you can get it right.'

'Hmmm ...' He pondered, rubbing his chin. 'Your dance recital costumes from that show you did.'

Ah, *those* costumes. Made of gold sequins from the time we'd tap danced as golden tickets. I shook my head. 'Even better. You're never gonna guess.'

'Ballerina Barbie?'

'Getting warmer, but it's even better than that.' I put him out of his misery, amused at the frown forming between his eyes. 'Our Pocket Pals!'

Jeez, his smile, when aimed in my direction, had my knees going weak.

'You loved those.' He chuckled. 'Thought Dad was gonna throw them in the ball return most days.'

'Oh, he definitely threatened to more than once.' The memory made me smile. 'Your dad always suffered the most from our obsessions.'

Dylan hummed in agreement.

'Dylan, I—'

'Are you planning—'

We both chuckled, the awkward reaction of two people going to ask something at the same time.

'You go first,' Dylan said.

I took a deep breath, ready to start a conversation I could use as a segue to ask him out.

Here goes nothing.

'Dylan, I was wondering—' My sentence was once again interrupted.

'Honeys!' a cheerful voice called up the stairs. 'I'm homeeeee.'

dylan

DAHLIA'S WIDE SMILE GREETED ME WHEN I reached the bottom of the stairs.

'Hey, looks like you've got a lot to do.' She nudged her head towards the still-open car boot. 'Need a hand?'

'If you don't mind,' I said, my body aware of Madison coming down the stairs behind me. Conscious of everything she did all the time. Deep down in my bones, her every movement was imprinted, and it scorched me. I needed to tamp it down—whatever *it* even was—so that I could be around her. 'Dottie here seems to have forgotten it's her crap we're hauling around.'

Dottie lifted her gaze from her phone and looked over to where the three of us were standing. 'I figured the two of you had it covered. Too many cooks and all that.'

'Right,' Madison said. 'You were thinking of the two of us. You're such a generous spirit, Dots.'

Dottie either didn't detect the sarcasm or chose to pay no attention to it. 'I am, aren't I?'

Dahlia ignored her. 'Once we've got the rest of the boxes in, want me to make something?'

'Ooh, yes, please!' Madison stepped around me and gave Dahlia a hug. The way her arms wrapped around her and squeezed made me wonder if she'd hug me with as much enthusiasm. An intrusive thought. Best kept locked up. 'You do have a way with pasta and cheese.'

'It is a skill of mine.' Dahlia wrapped her arm around Madison, and they went to sit on the sofa beside Dottie, who begrudgingly moved up to make room. 'How's your day been?'

'Well, Dottie and I spent a *lot* of hours sorting her room at your parents' place into keep and donate boxes. I'm sure I don't need to tell you how much there *wasn't* to donate.'

Dahlia nodded thoughtfully. 'Yes, Dot's always struggled with the concept of throwing things away.'

'You make me sound like a hoarder.'

'You make yourself sound like a petulant brat,' I said. Every time I glanced at Madison, I couldn't shake the uncomfortable feeling sitting in my gut. I'd acted like a dick earlier, telling her that in my head I still saw her as if she were ten. I hadn't seen her that way in a while, but especially not in the last week. Jeez, I could barely think about anything else *but* her.

It had been a while since I got laid, but honestly, that didn't even come into it.

Being around Madison had me questioning everything.

Madison stood abruptly. 'Okay, people. No more dilly-dallying. If we get a move on, we may be finished before midnight.'

'If we're lucky,' I agreed.

THE THREE OF us got all the boxes inside and up the stairs. Notice once again how Dottie did shit all. I'd never realised before how little she did and how much Madison did for her. I hadn't spent time around them in years, but has their dynamic always been like that?

'You two can handle it from here?' Dahlia asked with her hands on her hips, surveying Dottie's new kingdom. 'I'll force her to help me by getting her to grate cheese or something.'

'Thanks,' Madison said, her straight teeth on show. 'I think Dylan and I've got this. If Dottie wants things in a specific place, well, she'll be shit out of luck.'

Dahlia nodded, lips pursed. 'If you're sure.' She clapped her hands together. 'Okay, I'll call up when the food's ready.'

She left the room, and Madison and I each took a box from the centre, opened it up, and took out whatever lurked inside.

'I'm assuming the boxes don't have order?' I said, pulling out a scruffy ragdoll with red cheeks by her knit braid.

'Only the ones I did.' Madison pointed to the words written in black permanent marker on the box in front of her: CASUAL CLOTHES. 'Dottie, on the other hand ... pretty sure she threw things in with no rhyme or reason.'

'Sounds about right.' I took a deep breath, rubbing my temples with my fingertips. 'The kid pains me.'

Madison winced at my use of the word kid but took pity on me and changed the subject. 'Sorry, what were you about to say before ...?'

'Oh.' The question I'd been about to ask flew to the

forefront. 'I was going to ask if you'll be at the family tournament later this month.'

'As long as an event doesn't come up, yeah.' My eyes fixated on her hands as she took out each piece of clothing and set them down into different piles. 'I usually do.'

Huh. It had been a while since I'd attended one, but trying to think of the exact date threw me back.

'Why don't you come anymore?' she asked, focused on her task, separating trousers from T-shirts with ease. 'It's been ages since I've had the chance to beat you.'

'I suppose I hadn't realised how long it's been.' I breathed out through my clenched teeth. It was a subject I didn't linger on often, but the way her open face looked at me made me want to answer. Want to open up and talk to her more. A dangerous place to be. 'You remember Caroline?'

Madison nodded, still sorting the clothes, once more looking at them and not at me.

'Caroline didn't like to go bowling. Said it was silly and a waste of time.' Even saying the words had me questioning why I'd stayed with her so long. 'And any time I'd go without her, she'd guilt-trip me for leaving her to spend time with my family instead.'

'That sucks; I'm sorry.'

'Not your fault.' I turned my back to her, putting Dottie's multiple teddy bears and dolls on top of the chest of drawers. It was quite creepy, actually, with all their beady eyes staring blankly back at me. 'I should've known then that she and I weren't endgame.'

'You met at university, right?'

'Yeah. She studied architecture in the block next door to

law. For a long time, I believed it was love at first sight, but clearly, that's bullshit.' I shook my head, unsure why I was being so honest with her. I rarely think of Caroline these days. It was easier that way. 'Suppose you heard how it ended?'

Madison's wince told me she had.

It made sense. Not like Dottie had kept her opinion to herself when talking to me about it, so of course she'd have spoken to Madison about it, too.

Caroline cheated on me a year ago with a mate from secondary school. It blindsided me. I hadn't seen it coming —at all.

Afterwards, it became a little clearer.

I'd spent so much time at the office, working on The Syndicate case with Noah, that my relationship became something I didn't put enough effort into.

Every waking moment, my mind revolved around the case. The evidence. How to get it all to stick. Ways to argue, points to make, and so on.

Caroline was an afterthought.

Something she'd never been in her entire life and would never accept being without a fight.

Her cheating on me, in theory, should have been the wake-up call to spend less time at work and more time with my family, but that wasn't how it went.

If anything, I dived even deeper into working hard.

At first, I was gutted. Heartbroken. Unable to navigate through the foggy haze of despair.

But then it became a crutch. A way to stop my friends and family from setting me up on misguided blind dates for my "own good".

Noah asked me once if I still believed in love, and I told him I did, mainly because I hadn't wanted him to fuck things up with Hallie, whom he quite clearly adored.

But I wasn't sure. Maybe love wasn't in my future. Not until I'd reached my career goals, at least.

I turned back to face Madison looking up at me, a thoughtful expression on her face.

'Caroline and I weren't a good fit, that's all,' I said.

'Anyone you've got your eye on?' Madison's gaze met mine. 'Sure you get to meet all types of interesting people doing your job.'

Not like I could turn around and say, *Actually, Madison, I can't stop thinking about you.*

I shook my head in response, hoping she wouldn't pry further.

She smiled, but I couldn't make out her thoughts.

'Oh, while I remember,' I said, changing the subject swiftly away from anyone I may want. 'What were you about to ask before Dahlia came home?'

'Ah,' Madison said, her mouth moving down into a frown. 'I was just wondering ...'

She trailed off, her face one of deep concentration.

I waited, but she stayed still.

'Yes?' I nudged.

'Feel free to shut me down.'

Well, that was ominous.

'Okay ...'

'But I was wondering if you'd like to go on a date. With me.'

CHAPTER 7

madison

My heart stuttered, threatening to fly out of my chest, and with my luck, it'd hit Dylan in the face on its way out of the room, spattering him with blood and pieces of my insides.

The image dark, yet somehow comforting.

Dylan stopped moving. Stopped everything. Pretty sure he stopped breathing actually.

The hope, barely a spark, withered. The darkness beckoning from beyond.

Maybe me looking at him, all expectant, was causing him to freak out.

I looked back at the empty box in front of me and moved it to the bed out of the way. My fingers needed something to do, so I picked up the tee I'd placed on top of the pile and refolded it.

The wait excruciating.

The silence killing me.

'Say something,' I whispered, unable to stop myself. If

the answer was no, then it was no, but until he voiced it, I'd always wonder.

A croak left his throat.

Well, in all my teenage fantasies, he had never choked when I asked him out.

I opened my mouth, fully prepared to take the whole thing back when Dylan said 'no' and my heart died.

The rash I got when anxious crept up my chest, reaching my neck. I could feel it, all hot and itchy.

He didn't appear to sense my distress because the stupid man took a step closer to me before bending his knees and coming to eye level with me.

'Madison.' His pointer finger tilted my chin up. 'That came out harsher than intended.'

I blinked, frozen. My body hot at his touch but cold with fear at how the rest of the conversation would go.

'It's not that I don't want to go on a date with you. It's that I could never do that to Dottie.' He breathed out, the warmth of it fanning my face. 'Not to mention you're still a teenager and I turned thirty a few months ago.'

He smiled, half-joking, but I couldn't see past the phrase *still a teenager.*

The word stung.

Yes, I may be nineteen, but my twentieth birthday was less than two months away. I'd had to grow up fast in life, and I hated it when somebody tried to make me feel like a child who knew nothing of the world.

'Plus, after Caroline, I ...'

Dylan continued speaking, or at least his lips were moving, but no words entered my ears.

Only a low buzz, buzzing away, as a buzz was known to do.

Buzz, buzz, buzz.

'Madison, are you okay?' Sympathy shone in his gaze, and I wanted to die.

How could I have been so bloody stupid?

Of course Dylan would reject me.

My parents had.

Everybody but Dottie, the best friend a girl could have, and there I sat, asking her brother out, knowing she'd kill me for it.

My crush had turned me into a backstabbing best friend, and for what? A rejection.

I needed to get out of the room. Out of the house.

There was no other option available to me.

Without a word to Dylan, I fled.

◆

MY FEET TOOK me down the stairs at record speed.

No thought about how Dahlia and Dottie would react to me running down the stairs like I had a stampede of fans hot on my heels.

Dahlia's head popped out of the kitchen, serving spoon in hand, and gave me a quizzical stare. 'Everything okay, Mads?'

'Never better,' I replied, the epitome of easy breezy. 'Thanks so much for everything, but I've gotta be off now.'

'Are you sure everything's okay?' Dottie asked from the same place on the sofa she'd sat on since we arrived. Usually, I'd comment on her laziness, but it wasn't the time to. I

50

needed to get out of there before Dylan appeared. Or worse. Before he stayed away on purpose, which would kill me more than him appearing somehow.

My heart rate hadn't slowed.

Everything on high alert.

Run! Run! Run!

'But the pasta's nearly ready, and it's your favourite.'

'I'm not hungry,' I told Dahlia. 'I'll be over again soon, okay?'

'Do you want a lift?' Dottie asked, sitting a little straighter on the black fabric cushion. 'I don't mind, seeing as you've done the majority of the work today.'

'No, I'm good.' I didn't want to be stuck in a car with Dottie. Not after I'd all but betrayed her in her eyes. 'Fresh air will do me wonders and all that.'

I reached the door, my palm grasping the handle, when the footsteps of Dylan stirring upstairs banged through the ceiling.

If I stayed, he'd try to make things better, and I wasn't ready for that at all.

'Are you sure you're feeling okay?' Dottie's face scrunched up, a rare sign of care coming from her.

'Totally fine. See you later!' I practically shouted.

'Madison, wait!'

CHAPTER 8

madison

THE DOOR SLAMMED BEHIND ME.

It may as well have been the shutters of my heart.

How could I act so stupid and think I'd get away with it?

Of course Dylan wouldn't want to date me. Of course he wouldn't want to put his relationship with his sister in jeopardy for somebody like me.

Delusional cow.

And to use Caroline as one of his reasons? Fuck. He truly must find me pathetic.

My feet pounded on the pavement, the only sound around, and it hit me how late it had got without my noticing. Packed into the bedroom with Dylan in my vicinity, I'd lost track of everything.

A chill travelled through me, dampening the burn of anxiety and the rash still itching on my chest.

I'd left my jacket hung up on the coat hooks in my mad dash to leave, and the frigid February air entered my bones. *Stupid, stupid cow.*

My skin would blister and freeze before I got home, and it'd be all my fault, nobody else's.

What could make my journey home worse?

Yes. Rain.

Large, wet drops fell from the sky, coating my face and my body, and I laughed out loud at my predicament.

Voices travelled on the wind from up ahead, and I hated the idea of anybody seeing me in such a state. All my fingers and toes were crossed, hoping whoever I came across didn't follow me online, want a picture, or worse, to post a story.

I should've taken the lift from Dottie, potential awkwardness be damned.

Calm the fuck down, Madison.

It wouldn't do to spiral, and I was close to doing just that.

THE VOICES UP ahead grew louder as I got closer.

Shouting. Angry shouting.

Maybe it'd be best to avoid them, but no other route would get me home. The corner of Bottle Lane and Lake Avenue was where I could change route, but knowing my current luck, the bickering pair were there.

A child's playground sat on that corner and served as a meeting hub of sorts.

In fact, it was at that very park I first spoke to Dottie, back when she was five and I was six.

Quickly, it became clear I was about to stumble into the middle of a very heated argument.

Wonderful. Exactly what my evening needed. *Violence.*

The male voices, because they were definitely male, became distinguishable. Their words no longer unintelligible shouts.

'Look, Boss ain't happy with the way you handled it,' voice one said.

'I can get the money.' A second voice.

Two blurry figures emerged from the rain, and of course, they were standing on the corner of Bottle Lane and Lake Avenue, as I expected.

The Goddess of Luck had turned her back on me, leaving me out in the cold with nobody to turn to. Wow, rejected Madison acted maudlin.

'The money isn't all he cares about.'

'Malcolm, please,' the second guy said. 'I can get the money. Lawrence need never know.'

'You've left me with little choice.'

My feet continued taking me closer to the two figures up ahead, but every nerve ending in my body screeched at me to stop. Told me I needed to turn and run. Get away from whatever lay up ahead. The *danger* ahead.

'Malcolm, don't do this!'

The panic of the guy on the right hit me square in the chest. I wasn't about to walk across a simple disagreement, and bolting fast remained the only option left to me.

My feet moved. My body about to turn.

But then the person on the right, Malcolm, pulled a knife from his left pocket and stabbed it into the man in front of him. The one who'd begged him not to.

Huh. Rare to meet another left-handed person out in the wild.

The only explanation for that thought being my first

after watching somebody stab another human being was shock.

Pure and simple.

Malcolm stabbed again. And again.

I counted his hand stabbing and retracting at least ten times. Not quite enough to be classed as overkill, but still a bloody lot of times.

Shit.

Why did the term overkill enter my mind with such ease?

Shit.

Was I witnessing a murder? A real-life one and not one in a true crime documentary?

'Hey!' I shouted before my brain reminded me that I should stay silent and get the fuck out of there before being spotted.

Guess my mind and mouth were at war with one another. Per usual.

The assailant, Malcolm, dropped the knife at my holler. He ran off towards the alleyway, away from the bright lights of the town centre, leaving the other man to stumble and fall into a heap on the cold grey pavement.

I'd never been one to run fast, so it would do no use to follow him. Instead, I rushed to the man who'd fallen.

Maybe I could help him.

When his dark blood came into sight, I stopped and puked in the nearest bush. The acidic taste of vomit filling my mouth, highlighting how little I'd eaten all day.

I wiped my mouth with the back of my hand before I reached into my bag.

My phone in my hands.

999 pressed.

Dialled.

'999, which emergency service do you require?' the voice through my phone asked.

'Ambulance.' My heart rate skyrocketed. My skin cold and covered in goosebumps. Shit, should I have asked for the police? No. The man at my feet still had a chance, even with the blood pooling around him, leaking from the holes in his chest and stomach.

How had my evening taken such a dark turn?

When the ambulance dispatcher came on the line, I rattled off our location and what had happened. Hopefully, they'd alert the police, too.

'What can I do?' I shouted at the man, crouching down to assess the situation, completely lost to how I should act.

Emergencies never were my strong point.

My anxiety always got the better of me, and I crumbled. Completely useless. A wet fish. Or worse. A wet flannel. I laughed to myself. Now I really was losing it ...

'I've called the ambulance. They're on their way,' I said, talking to him like he could understand me. Like his eyes weren't rolling into the back of his head. His stare clouded.

The man's laboured breathing got worse with each intake of air into his lungs.

Shit. Shit. Shit.

If I'd taken the lift, I wouldn't be here.

Would never be able to bring the man dying at my feet, in front of my eyes, any justice.

Maybe that was why fate had me walk home.

Maybe there was a purpose to it all. A reason.

With one last ragged breath, the man at my feet uttered

his last words. I leaned down, my ear as close to his mouth as I could get it.

'Tell the police ...

'It was ...

'The Syndicate.'

CHAPTER 9

dylan

IN THE BLINK OF AN EYE, MONDAY MORNING CAME around, and I made my way into the office, not as bright-eyed and bushy-tailed as usual.

Ever since Madison fled my home on Saturday night, I couldn't stop thinking about her. About the way I handled it. I should have never let her leave.

'Morning, Dylan,' Dawn said from behind her desk. Her face looked smug, and I could tell she wanted me to ask what had made her so happy. At least one of us seemed cheerful.

'Morning! You're looking awful chipper this morning. Anything I should know about?'

'You'll be as happy as me when they tell you the news,' she said, her smile growing wider. 'Maybe even happier! Go on, get inside. I'm sure Noah's looking for you.'

I nodded and made my way inside.

Clearly, the other employees were aware of the good news because everyone was abuzz with gossip over at the drinks station.

A queue for the espresso machine always hinted at some drama going around.

'Morning,' I mumbled, grabbing two mugs from the top right cupboard.

'Morning,' they chirped back.

One of the new interns smiled at me. 'You just arrived?'

I nodded, shifting my weight to my left leg, hoping the awkward small talk wouldn't last too long. I never knew how to respond to keep it going.

'You heard the news? Bet Mick's having a field day.'

I shook my head. 'No, not yet.'

'Well, I'm sure Noah will find you soon.' She grinned and stepped aside from the coffee machine. 'Here you go.'

Something big must have gone down since I left the office on Friday night.

The espresso shots poured slowly into the cups, the thick aroma of coffee filling the air, and it grounded me.

Yes, the weekend threw me off, but I thrived on working hard. Being back at the office, news on the tips of everyone's tongues, set me alight in a way hard to explain.

Noah turned the corner that led down to the offices. 'Ah, you're here. Great.'

I handed him his mug and took a sip of mine; the coffee burned my throat on its way down.

'Meeting in the boardroom at ten.' Noah took a sip of his coffee. 'Some break in the case. Mick's buzzing about it.'

'Of course he is. It's what we've all been waiting for, isn't it?' I laughed, placing my empty mug down on the counter. 'This could be it.' I clapped Noah on the back. 'The body we need.'

'No idea what it is yet, but it's looking promising.'

'Maybe somebody's turned informant,' I said, thinking aloud. 'Not long until we find out.'

'Whatever it is,' Noah said, taking my empty mug and putting it in the dishwasher with his own. 'It can only be a good thing, right?'

THE LARGE BOARDROOM at the Taylor & Roberts office had a large glass wall that faced out across the communal areas of the office, with Dawn's desk visible if you angled yourself just right.

It baffled me why you'd want such an important meeting room to be visible to all, and I guessed Mick or Jeoffrey had that realisation too, as a year ago, they'd installed a new type of glass that could fog up at the touch of a button.

As me and the rest of the employees invited to the meeting filed in, the glass was still transparent, and once I took a seat, I watched as people went about their tasks. Lost in their own worlds.

A body plonked itself down into the seat to my right. 'Wanna know the hot juicy goss?'

My gaze turned to Eloise, the intern who would get offered a permanent position eventually, looking at me like the cat who ate the canary, the cream, and the cheese.

'The hot juicy goss?' I repeated, my chuckle unsure. Trust Eloise to make something serious sound like schoolroom chatter.

'Mhm.' She pursed her lips. 'Saturday night, some guy got stabbed.'

'Right ...'

'Oh, that's not the best part.' She looked around, leaned in, and lowered her voice. 'There's a witness.'

'Okay …'

I hated feeling stupid, but none of what she said added up in my head. A maths equation for which I had the two figures but no total.

'The guy who got stabbed'—she got even closer, the smell of coffee on her breath giving me pause—'was a runner for The Syndicate.'

Well, that changed things.

The excitement at the drinks station made sense. Dawn's smug smile, too.

Apparently, it was catching.

My nerves buzzed with something. A brief spark of light that certainly hadn't been there when I woke up.

'I assume that's what this meeting's about,' she continued, unaware of the fireworks she'd set off in my head.

I nodded and looked at my watch. 'Not long until we find out.'

More people filed in, taking their seats. Noah tilted his head, taking the seat opposite mine. My responding smile was wider than any I'd given in a long time.

This could be it.

Mick Taylor entered and took his position at the head of the long table. 'Okay, everyone. We're waiting on a few more people and then we'll begin.'

My gaze went around the room to pass the time.

Dawn, still smiling behind her desk, talking away to some blonde-haired woman.

Wait.

I recognised that head.

That hair.

I leaned back in my chair, trying to get a better view.

Madison?

Why would she be at Taylor & Roberts on a Monday morning?

'What's she doing here?' I asked aloud.

Maybe if I stretched back more. *Just a little further.*

The blonde woman turned, revealing Madison's beautiful face, a stark difference in appearance from a couple of nights ago when she'd fled from my place.

Just an inch more and I could get her attention.

dylan

My chair toppled, falling out from underneath me, and I splatted onto the floor at the same moment the boardroom door opened.

Dawn entered, with Madison behind her.

'Hello, everyone,' Mick said, his tone loud enough to draw everybody's attention away from me sprawled on the floor, bringing the meeting to a start.

Quickly, I scrambled back into my chair, the burn of my cheeks apparent.

Noah coughed, hiding his laughter.

'Everybody, this is Madison Jones, and she'll be sitting in on this meeting with us. All will become clear in time.'

Madison gave a hollow smile to the room, her makeup-less face looking tired. Worry pinched me.

'Hey,' Madison said before walking to the only empty chair in the room—the one to my left. She acknowledged me as she sat. 'Dylan.'

'What the fuck's going on, Mads?' I whispered out of

the side of my mouth, not wanting to draw attention to us. It sounded harsh, and I shouldn't have snapped at her.

'Shh,' she replied. 'We can talk after.'

Mick narrowed his gaze my way, and I sat up straighter in my chair.

Dawn left the room with a click of the door, and Jeoffrey pressed the button, turning the glass opaque.

Madison's signature scent overwhelmed me. God, she always smelled so good.

The thoughts I had towards her bordered on forbidden.

Of course, I couldn't think about my sister's best friend that way.

Especially with her sitting in my office, somehow now a piece of the puzzle that was The Syndicate case.

'Okay, let's begin, shall we?' Mick said as Jeoffrey took his seat at the end of the table. 'I'm sure the rumours and whispers have gone around this morning, but I'm here to tell you the facts.'

Everybody sat up a little straighter. Some shuffled the paperwork in front of them. We were all eager for whatever he had to say next.

'On Saturday night, around eleven p.m., Malcolm Silver stabbed a runner named Toby Scott on the corner of Bottle Lane and Lake Avenue.' He clicked the button on his remote, and an image of Toby Scott appeared on the screen behind him. 'The only witness'—he nodded towards Madison—'watched as Malcolm stabbed Toby ten times before he dropped the knife and ran away.'

The story whirled in my head.

I couldn't even comprehend how Madison must be feeling. My hand flexed, wanting so badly to reach out to her under the table, to give her my support. But I couldn't. Not after her running away from me. After I rejected her.

'Toby told Malcolm he could get the money and that Lawrence need never know.' Mick paced the front of the room, clicking his clicker so the presentation kept changing, showing more details to back him up. 'Madison Jones is our number one witness, our *only* witness, and we need to make sure this sticks.'

Madison fidgeted in her chair, her fingers playing with the hem of her skirt, and the urge to touch her only grew.

I needed to stay professional, but I burned to talk to her. To find out if she was okay. To make sure she was safe. Something I'd always wanted on some level or another.

Over the years, there were plenty of times when Madison had sought solace at our house as a way to escape her parents, and it always killed me to see her so lost and uncertain.

'Malcolm Silver will pay for his crime, and so will Lawrence Knight. That slippery bastard has put out his last hit,' Mick concluded. I'd missed the majority of what he said.

Noah kicked me under the table, tilting his head in Madison's direction.

I shook mine in response. We could talk about it later.

'Over the course of the week, I'll come and debrief you all one by one and let you know what's expected of you,' Mick said. 'But until then, I want you to continue working on the case as if this murder hadn't landed in our laps. You're dismissed.'

The words set the room into a blaze of conversation and movement.

People shuffled their belongings, placing them into a pile, ready to ferret them away to their desks. Others turned to their neighbour and whispered, the excitement of the turn in the case causing everyone to feel re-energised.

A fight waged inside me.

The break in the case—the thing we'd all been waiting for—filled me with joy. It was exactly what we needed.

But the reason I couldn't join in with my colleagues' enthusiasm? The fact Madison had witnessed something heinous to cause it.

My whole life, I'd wanted her to have the best. To break free from her parents and live her own life without fear or trauma.

She shifted beside me, her eyes lost, staring at the wall ahead.

Without thinking too deeply, I grabbed her wrist and pulled her up out of her chair, like a neanderthal claiming his prize.

'You're coming with me.'

madison

DYLAN'S OFFICE DOOR SLAMMED BEHIND US, AND he dropped my wrist.

I rubbed the area, soothing the ache he'd put there. Maybe he hadn't intended to grip me so tight, but the bruise of his fingerprints would be there either way.

Worry oozed off him.

We both stayed quiet, the heaviness of the morning catching up with us both.

I should've at least given him a heads-up. I could accept that. But every time I went to call or message him, I stopped myself.

He'd never actually given me his number, and I only had it because Dottie gave it to me once in case of an emergency.

'Are you okay?' he demanded, his eyes blazing.

My eyes stung from tears rushing to the surface. 'Are you mad at me?'

Pretty sure my bottom lip wobbled, too.

The idea he could be pissed off at me hurt. I didn't want

him to hate me for what I had, and hadn't, done. Didn't want him to think any of it was my fault.

My parents always told me everything was my fault, and the feeling of being a disappointment had stuck around long after they had.

The whispered question softened Dylan's gaze a little. 'I could never be mad at you, but I am worried.'

I took a deep breath, hating the way my stomach turned at his worry like a minor part of it was excited about it.

How fucked up.

'We were all worried,' he continued. 'Then we heard from Mum, of all people, you were no longer coming bowling.'

Ah, yeah. I had meant to apologise for not letting them know in my message to Dot, but by the time I remembered, it was way too late to bother her.

Dot lived for her beauty sleep.

'Why didn't you call? Why didn't you let us know?' The look on his face had my guilt rising. 'I would've come down to the station.'

He really was swoon-worthy when he acted the perfect gentleman.

'I was holed up at the police station for most of Saturday night and yesterday. I've barely had time to shower, let alone think.' I sighed, still too tired to function to the best of my ability. 'And the way we left things Saturday night ...'

He winced. 'You could've told Dot about it when you messaged her yesterday.'

I nodded. 'I know, I'm sorry. The police had my phone, and by the time I got home, I didn't want to rehash it all again. Honestly, the idea of sleep had me in a chokehold I couldn't untangle myself from.'

'What happened?' he asked, taking a step closer to me. 'I barely heard Mick in there. I was so focused on you. Are you sure you're alright?'

'I'm okay,' I whispered, my tears spilling over. The emotions hadn't fully hit yet, but there was only so long I could keep them at bay. 'I don't think I'm ready to talk about it yet, though. I had to repeat myself so many times for the police, then for your bosses. I promise I'll talk to you when I'm ready.'

He nodded. He wouldn't push me. That wasn't Dylan's style. No matter how much he wanted to know more.

It all made sense to me now. How hard he worked. How dedicated he was to the case. All of a sudden, I'd joined the inner sanctum of his brain, as it were. Knew more than his family even.

So many times, Dottie or Dahlia had spoken about how little they knew of his case. How secretive he was about the work he did.

Shit.

The chance laid out before me was one I'd wanted for a long, *long* time.

Witnessing what I had gave me a reason to spend more time with Dylan. To make him finally like me for who I am *now* and not as the kid he once knew.

A sharp thrill shot through me.

My face remained solemn.

Dylan came closer again, only an inch of space between us. 'I'm so sorry for how we left things on Saturday. For how I acted. I should've come after you, not let you slam the door and leave.' He looked into my eyes. 'I'm going to regret it forever, Mads.'

My stomach tumbled the way it always did when he used my nickname. The way his lips moved when he uttered the name *Mads* sent me into overdrive. How could one man be so bloody gorgeous?

Truly, it was a crime.

The way he said my name had me amped up, my heart rate spiking, and I opened my mouth to say something—anything—when one of his bosses burst through the door, shattering the moment.

'Dylan,' he barked. 'I need an audience with you.' He took one look at me before returning his unimpressed gaze to Dylan. 'Now.'

dylan

JEOFFREY SAT BEHIND HIS DESK AS MICK PACED IN front of me.

I stood, my hands clasped in front of my waist, waiting for them to tell me whatever they'd interrupted my conversation with Madison for.

I hated leaving her there, tears in her pretty eyes. All I wanted was to open my arms to her and pull her close. Hug her tight and breathe in her scent like an animal.

Maybe it was a good thing Mick had pulled me out of there before I did something I couldn't take back. Something that would confuse everything.

'I'm sorry for bursting in,' Mick said, rubbing his jaw. 'Clearly, you and Miss Jones have a history together. Anything we should know about?'

'What do you mean?' I asked, not wanting to speak before I spun it to sound a lot better than my initial response, which was something like: *if you must know, I can't stop thinking about her eyes, her smile. The way she lights up any room she walks into.*

Yeah, that wasn't what they needed to hear. Ever.

'I mean,' he said, enunciating each word so it sounded like a full stop came afterwards, 'do the two of you have a romantic relationship? Or any kind of relationship that could fuck this up for us all?'

I shook my head. 'No. She's my younger sister's best friend, that's all. They've known each other since they were little. We're ... acquaintances, I suppose you'd say.'

'And?'

'And?'

'And is there something going on between the two of you? Because when I came into your office, the two of you were standing mighty close for two people who are mere acquaintances.'

'I promise, Mick. There's nothing more to it than that. Until my sister's birthday party the other week, I hadn't seen her in years.'

It seemed best if I stayed quiet about Saturday and how she'd fled from my house before stumbling across Malcolm and Toby's altercation.

'You make sure it remains that way.' Mick stopped pacing, thank fuck, because he'd started to make me nauseous. 'We can't have anything ruining this for all of us, so make sure you keep it in your trousers, all right?'

Why was it the moment he mentioned keeping it in my trousers, the more I wanted to *not* keep it in my trousers?

'That settles that,' Jeoffrey said, having stayed quiet while Mick paced. The two of them were equal partners in the firm, but Mick always got involved first. To talk first, think later.

Jeoffrey was the quieter one. The one who thought

things through before making a decision. Nobody would describe him as impulsive, that was for sure.

'Winters,' Jeoffrey said, clasping his palms in front of his chest as he leaned back in his large black leather chair. 'What Mick is trying to say here is we need you to keep the girl close. Dramatic as it may be, she's our last hope.'

I swallowed the extra saliva gathering in my mouth.

'She's in danger now. The Syndicate, when they catch wind of this, of what she knows, will want her dead.' Mick paced again. 'Seeing as you already know her, it makes sense for you to stick close. Originally, we thought to ask Noah, but this will work out better for everyone.'

The words swirled. Little did they know I'd rejected the poor girl a mere two days ago and chances were she wouldn't take lightly to being forced to spend time with me.

Or worse.

It would give her false hope of more.

Scratch that. Even worse would be me falling for her. Wanting to spend more time with her. Something that cannot happen under any circumstances.

With my job on the line, I couldn't let my potential feelings for Madison Jones be the reason everything turned to shit.

Even if her lips were like a siren's call.

Jeoffrey frowned, a bushy silver eyebrow turning down from behind his desk. 'Can you do it, Winters? Can you keep the girl by your side?'

'Yes,' I said with a decisive nod. 'I believe I can.'

madison

Two days had passed since I'd sat in the boardroom of Taylor & Roberts and tried to keep my cool with Dylan Winters sitting beside me, in a grey suit no less.

Was there literally anything he didn't look good in?

Even sitting on my old, haggard sofa, he looked so fucking hot my vision threatened to blur.

Damn him.

I handed him a glass of water and sat on the sofa beside him. If there'd been another spot to take, I would've, but my living room was quite small. Like the rest of my flat, come to think of it.

'You okay?' I asked, still shocked he'd shown up at mine.

He took a sip, looking around the bare room. I owned little, and until that moment, it didn't bother me, but watching his eyes look at the empty space filled me with something awful close to shame.

'Yeah, you?'

I chuckled. 'Bit of a loaded question that, isn't it?'

He laughed, too. 'Suppose it is. I'm sorry I couldn't be

here earlier, but I needed to go into the office and sort some stuff out.'

'That's okay. Not like I expect you to babysit me or anything, Dill.'

The nickname rolled off my tongue the way it always had. All the Winters called him Dill. Most people thought it was a shortened version of his name, but actually, it was a shortened version of dill pickle because of how much he loved them growing up. People in England call them gherkins, of course, but he'd learned the term dill pickle on a US TV show and refused to call them gherkins ever after.

'My bosses want me to do just that actually.' His wry smile sent shooting stars in my direction. 'You're to stay in my sight at all times.'

'That feels a little invasive,' I joked. 'Am I allowed to shower alone, or ...'

'I'm pretty sure your bathroom usage wasn't included.'

'Well, thank the heavens for that, ay?' Although, if he did want to shower with me, I wouldn't say no ...

'Really, Mads.' He angled his body to mine, and I did the same. 'How are you? We haven't had much chance to talk about all this.'

'What's there to say?' I took a sip of my water, needing to do something with my hands, the cool glass calming me down. 'I'm okay, I promise. Obviously, it's all come as a bit of a shock.' I froze, the mental image of Toby lying in a pool of his blood at my feet. 'I don't think it'll ever go away,' I whispered.

'What you witnessed?'

I nodded. 'His open eyes, forever staring into my soul. Questioning me. Wondering about me.'

'I know this isn't the same as being there or anything,' he said, taking a deep breath, 'and I don't want you to think I'm trying to negate your experience or anything like that.'

I waited, no idea how he'd finish his rambling.

'But I looked at the pictures from Saturday night.' Dylan blinked, but I stayed silent. 'It's completely understandable why you can't get it out of your head.'

'Yeah. Your bosses have arranged for counselling actually. So that's pretty good of them, seeing as they don't have to do shit for me.'

Dylan blurted out, 'It's my fault.'

'Huh?'

'It's my fault you stumbled across what you did. That you're now involved in something I'd hoped to keep well away from my family.'

If he continued speaking, it wasn't in English or anything decipherable because the moment he'd called me family I zoned out. Fuck, I liked the way it sounded, especially from his lips.

'Dill, don't be silly. Of course this isn't your fault.'

'But if—'

'I'd really rather we didn't.' I cut him off. 'Just know I don't blame you at all. It's not like *you* stabbed anyone.'

'Mads.' He tried again, his hand grabbing mine. Sparks flew.

'Seriously,' I said, taking my hand slowly out of his, not wanting to tempt fate—or myself—further. 'Let's move on from it. Especially if we've got to spend time together.'

'If you're sure?' His face said the opposite.

'I am.'

He nodded, accepting the finality in my tone. 'Okay.

Well, I'm sorry you're gonna get dragged to the office with me a couple of times a week for a bit.'

'Not like I've got anything better to do.' I shrugged. 'I'm not allowed to post online until this is all over.'

'But that could be years.'

I gritted my teeth. 'I'm fully aware, yes.'

'Shit.'

'Yep.' I let out the breath I held. 'It's a relief in a way, honestly.'

'How so?'

'Well, I've never exactly *liked* doing it.' The index finger of my left hand fiddled with the ring I always wore on my right hand. 'I stumbled into it ...'

'I remember.' He laughed. 'Dottie couldn't believe it when people cared about your clothes and the way you style your hair.'

'I know you think it's silly.' I smiled at him, catching him off guard. No, he'd never outright said so, but I knew him well enough to know he wouldn't view it as a career or anything worthwhile. 'Trust me, I did at the start, too. Until I realised it could mean having enough money to leave my mum.'

'Does she still reach out?'

I shook my head. 'No, and thank fuck for that because I don't want to be near the woman ever again.'

'That's understandable. Did you leave after your dad died?'

'Yep.' It was rude of me to act so blunt, but fuck, I hated talking about my parents.

'I know I said it before—'

'If you're about to apologise about my dad again, I might actually hit you. He was a waste of space, Dill.'

'But he was still your dad.'

I laughed, the sound bitter even to my own ears. 'The fact you said that with a straight face tells me a lot about your relationship with your own parents.'

'You already know all about my relationship with my parents,' he said, and I hummed in agreement. 'Does your mum still live in Lakeland?'

'I assume so. I've never heard otherwise.' A road of conversation not worth driving down. 'Don't think I'll be in Lakeland much longer if I can't work. Can't exactly pay for this place without money.' I gestured around at my empty place. Sure, it wasn't much, but it was mine. Sort of.

'We'll figure something out,' Dylan said with such certainty I couldn't do anything but believe him. Over the course of our talk, he'd moved closer. 'I won't let you lose this place.'

His breath fanned my face, and our eyes locked together.

One inch more and we'd be close enough to kiss ...

dylan

THE SKY OUTSIDE THE LARGE GLASS WINDOW, darker than usual, was lit only by the lights of the city in the distance.

The view from my office always made me stop and stare.

One of the many perks of the job.

Yet my thoughts, instead of being on the view, were on mine and Madison's almost-kiss. We were at her apartment, faces inches from touching, yet I'd backed away at the look of longing on hers. I didn't want to lead her on by kissing her until I knew my feelings.

Madison came to work with me, as she had since Monday, and I liked having her around. The day had turned into evening a lot faster than expected, and it made sense to grab food to eat at the office rather than wait until after we made it back to Lakeland.

Madison walking into my office had me turning around away from the view, and I went to help her with the containers grasped in her small arms.

'Pretty sure the entire office ordered one of everything

off the menu.' She paused so I could take some bits from her. 'Delivery guy seemed highly amused.'

'We always order from the same place, so I think they're used to it now.'

'Does this happen often?' she asked, placing the last of the food down on my desk for the two of us to dish up.

'The entire office ordering takeaway? A lot more than it should, yeah. We cycle through different cuisines, though. Mix it up a bit.'

'And of course I happen to be here for Chinese night.'

'At this rate, you're gonna be here for a lot of different nights. Do you not like Chinese?'

'It's not my fav,' she said but opened the closest container with relish. 'But at this point, I'm so starved it wouldn't matter if you put a beef burger in front of me.'

'But you detest beef burgers.'

'Exactly!' she said, pointing a chopstick my way. 'It's my fault for not eating lunch ... or breakfast actually, come to think of it.' She shook her head, her blonde hair swishing with the movement. 'I should set myself alarms to remind myself to eat.'

Madison looked at the food on my desk and then at the floor.

'You know what? I think we should put everything on the floor and pick and choose what we want.'

'You trying to steal some of my chicken chow mein?'

'You know I am.' She stuck her tongue out. 'If I have to eat Chinese, then you bet I'm having your chow mein.'

'Then why didn't you order your own?'

'Because I knew you'd be ordering it.' The *duh* implied.

'Touché.'

We settled on the floor and dished up, our conversation dwindling the second food hit our taste buds.

'Mmm,' she moaned, and the sound went straight to my core.

I crunched down on a prawn cracker that tasted like cardboard but continued eating as if they didn't taste like dirt-covered ash, mainly so I had something to do to take my focus off wanting her.

We both fell into a comfortable silence, eating our food and brushing hands every time we both reached for the same container.

Finally, after we were both stuffed, Madison smiled and said, 'Do you remember the time Dean pranked Dahlia—'

Mads's random outbursts always made me smile. She'd go quiet for a bit, then come out with some memory or statistic, all because her brain wouldn't stay quiet.

My laugh was automatic, the image of Dahlia covered in blue paint is still amusing nearly ten years later. It hit me that I knew the time she referred to without her saying it, like we were in sync.

'Wait,' I said. 'We are talking about the time Dahlia became a Smurf, right?'

'1000 per cent.' Madison laughed. 'I honestly thought she was gonna kill him.'

'Think Mum hid him for the rest of the night so she couldn't.'

'It's like the time Dana cut up Dottie's favourite skirt. Your mum literally arranged for me and Dottie to stay at her best friend Cara's house so Dana would survive the night.'

The memory didn't ping for me. 'Ah, I must've been too

old by then. Thought it made me uncool to hang out with you younger kids.'

'Ah, yeah, maybe.'

Ever since our near-kiss the other day in her flat, I'd tried to keep a good distance between us. A physical distance, at least. I still needed to be with her, and it wouldn't do to make shit awkward between us. Not when we could have months together before any kind of case is thrown at Malcolm Silver.

They needed to find the fucker first.

He'd gone underground, no doubt hidden by his father, or some other person loyal to The Syndicate. And with their code of silence, I doubted anybody would spill willingly.

Madison took my plate from my lap and placed it on top of hers.

'I can tidy up,' I said, brought out of thoughts of Malcolm and where he could be.

'There's no need,' she said, waving me off. 'You already do enough for me. I'm the one who sits around here all day making the place look untidy.'

'You could never make anything look untidy, Mads.'

The smile she sent in my direction caught my breath.

She really was so fucking beautiful. So full of life.

And if I allowed myself to think of her in that way, with no barriers or limits, I could see myself falling in a way too dangerous to contemplate.

madison

IT WAS A COMPLIMENT, RIGHT?

You could never make anything look untidy, Mads.

It had to be.

Dylan Winters wasn't one to say things he didn't mean, and so the logical leap was he was being nice to me.

My insides fluttered, the butterflies in my stomach whenever I was around him going full speed.

I put the empty containers and plates on his desk before taking my spot back beside him on the floor.

Surprisingly, the carpet had a bounce to it that made it rather comfortable.

Dylan tilted his head.

I scooted a little closer to him, only a fraction, close enough that the lighter flecks in his brown eyes shone.

'Bowling on Sunday,' I said. 'You ready to get your arse beat?'

Bonnie had postponed the February meeting so I could attend. Even though I hadn't messaged Dylan or Dottie while at the police station, I'd texted Bonnie to let her know I wouldn't be able to make bowling.

My priorities were a little screwed, clearly. I just never wanted Bonnie to think I didn't appreciate her, or care about her.

He laughed. 'You think you can beat me, for real? I'm the champion bowler.'

'You are not!' I poked him on the shoulder. 'Dean is, but he's not around to prove you lie.'

'Does he ever contact you?'

'Sometimes. He's loving all of it.' It had been a couple of weeks since I'd last spoken to Dean Winters. His band was touring Europe, and he had little time to keep up with every-one's messages. 'Do you not?'

'Dean and I aren't the closest,' Dylan said, rubbing his jaw. 'Everyone always assumes we are because we're the only boys.'

'There's an age gap between you though,' I pointed out, regretting it the moment it left my lips. The bigger age gap between me and him was something I didn't want to remind him of, especially not when we were sitting so close together.

'Only seven years.'

My heart grasped his *only* and held it tight.

'You've also not got much in common,' I continued. 'I'm sure if you messaged, he'd get back to you ... in like a month's time or so.'

Dylan waved me off. 'It doesn't matter. I'm honestly happy he's living the life he's always wanted to have.'

'All your siblings are.'

He hummed in thought. 'Yeah, suppose you're right. Dahlia's got the salon, and Dana adores working at the library surrounded by all those musty books, plus, Dottie loves attention, so stumbling across social media must've made her entire life.'

He wasn't wrong.

'Your parents are super proud of you all,' I said. 'I know they are. Your mum tells me all the time.'

'You and my mum are close.' He said it as a statement rather than a question.

Bonnie's warm smile popped into my head, and it made me smile.

'We are,' I confirmed. 'Bonnie's the best. She's always been there for me. I could never repay her for all she's done, ya know?'

For as long as I could remember, Bonnie had never treated me any differently from her other children, and I'd always looked at her as a surrogate parent. Same with Mike. They were my found family, and I'd fight like hell to make sure it always stayed that way.

'She's always looking out for you.' Dylan moved an inch closer, his fingertips spread on the floor beside him. Our little fingers grazed, the spark between them nearly sending me into overdrive. I looked to his face for a reaction and found none. 'Mum, and Dad actually, have always viewed you as another daughter. They're proud of you, too.'

Tears filled my eyes. Making them proud, having them be proud of me, it meant a lot.

'Talking of your mum, she messaged me to double-check about Sunday. Did you tell her about ...'—I gestured around his office—'all of this?'

He shook his head.

'I've told her as much as I can without breaking the

many confidentiality clauses I signed back at the beginning before knowing it'd take the turn it has. She knows about you witnessing a murder, though.'

'Oh.' I leaned back against the wall, hovering my head near his shoulder. Another centimetre and it'd be resting on him. 'I should've called her, but I was scared she'd admonish me for walking home alone. Plus, I didn't exactly wanna tell her *why* I'd refused a lift home and ran out of your house like the hounds of hell were snapping at my heels.'

Dylan looked down. I looked up.

It was like the other night on my sofa all over again, our faces close enough that if I reached up the slightest bit, our lips would touch.

His breathing sped up.

Fuck it. You only live once and all that.

Go for it, Mads.

So I stretched my neck and placed a soft kiss on his perfect lips.

Sparks flew. Fireworks burst on the back of my eyelids when I closed my eyes and moved my lips against his.

Until his lips were no longer on mine. No longer taking part in the same dance.

The fireworks sputtered out.

I leaned back, tentatively opening my eyes to Dylan's torn gaze, looking down at me.

'Mads,' he croaked. 'We can't.'

I blinked up at him, waiting for the rest of his rejection.

So stupid of me to think my actions would lead to anything *but* another rejection.

'It's not that I don't want to,' he whispered. 'But there are too many reasons why we can't. There's the case, my job,

Dot.' He stressed the last point harder than the rest. 'I need to stay professional.' He reached out and brushed a strand of my hair away from my face; the touch was gentle yet pointed. 'Not to mention you're basically an honorary Winters and the fallout from everybody ...'

He trailed off, and it became obvious to me how he viewed me.

A little sister.

One of the family.

Even if a tiny part of him wanted to kiss me, he didn't plan to explore it.

My chest itched, the red rash of rejection climbing up my neck to my face.

I stood, brushing down my skirt before going to his desk and grabbing the empty plates.

'I'll take these to the dishwasher.'

'Madison,' Dylan said, standing too.

I shook my head, not wanting another word to come out of his stupidly perfect face. 'We should head back to Lakeland. It's getting late.'

The door of his office loomed ahead, blurred through the tears in my vision.

Tears I didn't want Dylan to see.

I'd done all I could, and now I needed to move past my ridiculous childhood crush on Dylan Winters.

madison

LAKELAND LANES ALWAYS COMFORTED ME.

After having a bad day, I could come here and relax. Any worries or fears floating away the moment I put on a pair of used bowling shoes.

Dahlia manned the shoe counter for us, taking our shoes and handing over the bowling ones in their place.

Dana and Dottie were standing next to me, both of them leaning on the counter, watching Dahlia's every movement.

They were suspicious of her, mainly because they worried she'd give them a pair taken from an unlucky number cubby-hole. Or worse, give them a pair with Velcro that had seen better days.

'Ah,' Dahlia said, placing a pair of size sixes in front of me. 'Are you truly bowling if you don't wear shoes other people have put their trotters in?'

'Please never say the word *trotters* again,' Dottie said, her face crumbling in distaste.

'What's wrong with saying trotters?' Dahlia laughed. 'You got something against trotters, Dot?'

'You are the worst.' Dottie turned away haughtily and headed to the red benches.

Dahlia rolled her eyes, and Dana sniggered beside me. Being around the three of them always made my day so much brighter.

'She thinks she's a real-life princess,' Dana said, her gaze following Dot's flounce. 'Can imagine her head's a mine-field.' She thought further about it before adding, 'Or a vacuous pit.'

'Did she tell you she bumped into Nathan again the other day?' Dahlia whispered, leaning closer to me and Dana across the counter. 'While she was out with, oh, what's-his-name?'

'Braydon,' I supplied, remembering Dottie's emphasis the last time we spoke about her love life.

'Right, him.' Dahlia came around the counter, a pair of shoes in her grip. 'Well, apparently, Nathan was with Lee, who is now dating Sophie.'

Dana and I gasped, the gossip fuelling us.

'Lee and Sophie?' Dana shook her head. 'Never saw that one coming.'

Dahlia nodded in agreement.

'What's the holdup?' Dottie hollered from the bench, shoes already on her feet, ready to go. 'If we don't get started soon, we won't finish until midnight.'

'Dot, it's only like half eight.' I went and sat beside her. There was nothing like putting on bowling shoes. They grounded me the moment they were tightly fastened on my feet.

Dana and Dahlia moved to the bench opposite us.

'So Mads.' Dahlia swung her acute gaze my way. 'How are you holding up? Dill won't tell us much, but he told us the main points.'

'Are you forever traumatised?' Dottie hushed, worry on her features. 'It sounds positively ghastly.'

'I suppose I've not processed it all yet,' I said. 'It's all still super surreal, you know? Like I dreamed it or it happened to somebody else, somehow. But the police and the law firm have been so good about everything. Dylan, too.'

'I hope you're not getting ideas now that you're spending all this time with our brother, Madison,' Dottie said, eyebrows as pointed as the statement. 'Because I would never forgive you if you so much as looked at him with lustful thoughts.'

Lustful thoughts? If only she knew the truth.

I rolled my eyes in response, hoping my face didn't flush and give me away. 'We hang out at a law office in the city. He works and I don't. Nothing to talk about here.'

Dahlia and Dana remained quiet, watching me thoughtfully.

Must break the tension.

'We should go to Carillo's,' I said. 'I haven't been in ages, and nowhere sells a burger quite like theirs.'

'How would you know?' Dana laughed. 'You don't eat beef.'

'I'll rephrase,' I said. 'Nowhere sells a *chicken* burger quite like theirs.'

We all laughed.

'It's a date,' Dana said. 'I've got so much to fill you girls in on.'

My eyes strayed over to where Dylan stood at the bar with his mum. Like a sixth sense, I always sensed his presence, no matter where he was in the room.

'Ew.' Dottie leaned in to whisper in my ear. 'Can you stop watching my brother like that? Creeper.'

Do not respond. Do not respond.

I stood, dragging my eyes away from Dylan. 'Let's go bowl.'

NO MATTER WHAT, we bowl on lanes seven and eight.

They were the two lanes in the centre of the alley, and nobody could explain why, but they were lucky.

Dana stepped up to the machine in the centre of the seating area, the ball return in front of her, ready to input our names into the system.

Of course, you couldn't use your *real* name.

You had to use an alias. Or some funny name somebody else suggested for you.

No name could be repeated at a later date. Everything must be new and original, meaning Dylan couldn't be Dill Pickle.

'Right, who's got a good 'un?' Dahlia rubbed her hands together, a wicked gleam in her eyes.

'I've got an idea,' Dottie said. 'Why don't we use our favourite film characters or bands or something? Don't think we've ever done that before.'

'We have not,' I agreed. 'Okay. So Dottie is obviously Regina. I'll be Gretchen.' Dottie and I nodded at each other, totally on the same wavelength, the way we usually were. It wouldn't do to think about the real-life comparisons, or about how being Gretchen to somebody's Regina wasn't always a good thing.

'Okay,' Dana said, inputting the names. 'We'll go from youngest to oldest.'

'Well, then you have to be Matilda.' Dahlia nudged Dana, who put the name in without question. 'I, of course, will be Eliza.'

I smirked. Eliza was the main character in Dahlia's favourite film, *Rules of Engagement*, starring Jackson James and Bridger Daniels. She'd denied even liking it when we watched it in the cinema, but clearly, she'd lied.

Dana input Sister Helen as Dylan's name, Jane for Bonnie, and finally, Jason for Mike.

'Done,' Dana said, pressing the button to start the game. 'Now, just got to wait for these losers to come over with our drinks.'

Once more, my eyes sought out Dylan. Things were still a little awkward after the kiss in his office, but the day after, we pretended nothing had happened and went back to ignoring the blatant sexual tension brewing between us both. Easier that way.

His eyes locked with mine, and I melted.

dylan

EVEN FROM ACROSS THE ALLEY, I COULD SENSE Madison's gaze on me, like a laser.

She and my sisters were over by the benches, putting on bowling shoes, the four of them no doubt in cahoots.

'Madison looks to be doing okay, all things considered,' Mum said, following my gaze. I hummed. 'I assume you still can't tell me or your father more about what you're working on?'

I shook my head. Mum had made it clear she wanted to know but because she respected me, she never pushed. A good thing really because knowing me, I'd blurt it all if she pried too deep. Bonnie Winters could interrogate anybody and get results.

'Dylan,' she said, her tone one to be wary of.

'Mum.'

I looked over to Madison, now over by the lanes with the girls, the four of them giggling as they put names into the system. Lord knew what they'd come up with this time. Last time I'd shown my face at a family tournament, I'd been called Stinky Pete the whole evening.

She turned, her eyes locking with mine, a faint blush rising onto her cheeks. I wanted to reach out and touch her soft skin, feel her. Be near her.

Our near kiss had me thinking of nothing else, so now I had an actual kiss to think about? I couldn't stop replaying it in my head over and over.

As much as I wanted to go to her, I remained where I stood with Mum, hoping nobody else spotted the longing on my face.

'Well, I've been thinking about this mess with Madison, and I think it'd be for the best if you moved in with her.' Her small brown eyes widened, a plea hidden within them. 'Just until this is all resolved, and her safety can be guaranteed again without constant supervision.'

'Mum,' I said, not knowing how to tell her it was a bad idea for me to be around Madison for any longer than I already was. 'I can't insert myself into her home without invitation. Her life's been upended by all this enough as it is.'

'I know, I know.' She reached out her hand, and I let her grasp mine. 'I'm just so worried about her. What if she's a target now because of what she saw?' Little did she know how close to the truth she lingered. 'I can't have anything happen to her, Pickle. Somebody needs to keep an eye on our girl, and I can't think of anybody more suited to that than you.'

I stayed quiet. Could I live with her? Could I watch her go to bed in the evening, be the first person around when she woke, and keep myself away from her? Prevent myself from doing the one thing I couldn't stop thinking about—kissing her. Touching her skin.

Mum, thankfully unable to view the salacious images in my head or the things I wanted to do to Mads, squeezed my hand. 'Madison's family.' She smiled, watching as Dottie and Madison threw some practice bowls on lane seven. 'And family matters more than anything.'

'Doesn't it make more sense for her to move in with me, Dottie, and Dahlia safety-wise?' Mum knew full well that it did.

Her lips pursed together. 'Sure it does, dear, but it'll be too crowded with all four of you. Plus, Dottie wouldn't leave her alone.'

Her unspoken sentence hovered in the air.

And if Dottie doesn't leave her alone, then you won't get to spend time with her.

WITH ONLY THREE more frames to go, Madison and I were tied.

'You're going down, Winters.' Madison walked to the ball return, bending down to pick up her trusty purple sixteen-pound ball, and my eyes strayed to her behind. Dahlia coughed, and I looked up to find her raised eyebrows. I shrugged and looked away.

Mads bowled, knocking down all ten pins. She blew on her knuckles as she walked back to take her place beside Dottie on the booth seating.

'A pure fluke,' I said. An untruth. The girl had bowled

four strikes, and she meant business. 'Highly doubt you can replicate it.'

'That a challenge?' she asked, leaning around Dot to look at me. 'Because I challenge you to get a strike on your turn, arsehole.'

Everyone laughed, and Dana got up to take her turn.

Had Madison always fit in so easily? I couldn't remember a time without her around, a time when she'd been an outsider.

Why had it taken me so long to notice her?

Obviously, the near-eleven-year age gap between us had something to do with it.

By the time the last frame came around, I was ready to leave.

Not because I didn't want to spend time with my family, but because I couldn't watch Madison getting along with my family any longer.

It was like a veil had lifted, and I could finally view beyond to see the truth right in front of me.

How often had I wished Caroline would get along with my sisters? Would enjoy bowling and spending time together while around my family?

But I always made excuses for her.

Or made excuses to not come to the lanes at all.

I hated thinking back to the way I'd acted and the way I'd put her above my family, even when it sat wrong in my gut.

Madison finished the game with a flourish. 'That's another two strikes for me. I'm on fire tonight!'

Cheers went up throughout our group.

'You haven't won yet,' I said. 'Never a good look getting too cocky, Madison.'

'Oh, but Dill Pickle.' She sent a cheeky smile my way. 'You'd have to get three strikes to beat me, and I don't see a turkey in your future.'

'And what *do* you see in my future?'

She paused, the tension in the air thick. Could anybody else sense it, too?

'Can't go and give out all my secrets, can I?' She laughed, swivelling her head to Dahlia, who had finished her turn, now returning with a smug smile on her face. 'You're up.'

I made my way to the ball return and picked up my usual light-blue ball, walked to the line, and bowled a perfect arc. It was magnificent.

So cocky I'd bowled a strike, I turned around to watch Madison's reaction, rather than the lane.

The look on her face didn't disappoint when the pins crashed down one by one.

'Well done,' she said, her smile catching. 'Now do it again.'

So I did.

Her smile became brittle, all gritted teeth, with no warmth left lurking in her eyes.

My hand shook as I waited for my ball to come back up the chute. Madison wouldn't appreciate it if she thought I let her win, but at the same time, I wanted to behold the joy that'd cover her face if she beat me. What to do?

My body ran on autopilot when it came to bowling. No way to throw my shot, even if I wanted to.

The ball rolled down the lane. It spun. It curved.

It ... didn't knock down all ten pins.

Shoot.

Madison's cackle reached me before I could even turn around to observe her exact level of smugness. 'Victory is mine!'

My family cheered, hollering and clapping as if she'd won something bigger than our monthly game.

'Congratulations,' I said, putting my hand out for her to shake.

'GG,' she said, taking my hand and shaking it with a firm grip. *Good game.*

Dad clapped her on the shoulder. 'What's our winner drinking?'

'Just a Diet Coke, please, Mike.'

Dad went off to the bar, and—much too slowly for my liking—the rest of my family followed him.

'Come on,' Madison said, brushing her hair back. 'Let's get you a drink, loser.'

My mum's words from earlier looped in my head. I would never forgive myself if any harm came to Madison, which meant there was only one logical next step for the two of us.

She turned as if to walk away from me and head over to the bar, when I put my hand out to stop her.

'Mads, wait,' I said, taking a deep breath, preparing myself for the worst. 'I've been thinking.'

Her eyes crinkled at the edges. 'Yes?'

'Can I move in with you?'

madison

LIFE ALWAYS TOOK A TURN WHEN YOU LEAST expected it.

Somehow, within less than a month, I'd gone from seeing Dylan for the first time in years at his sister's party to having him move in with me to keep an eye on me because I'd witnessed a murder that could get me in trouble with some super bad people.

A knock on my door had me dragging my feet to open it.

Yes, I was excited to have Dylan staying, but after his multiple rejections, it also filled me with dread.

Being around him, wanting him the way I did, but knowing I couldn't act on it was akin to torture in my eyes.

But of course, I opened the door.

Dylan stood there, still in his work suit, a large bag hanging from his arm and one singular cardboard box on the floor at his feet.

My ground-floor maisonette wasn't big enough for him to have his own wardrobe, let alone his own room, so it made sense he didn't have much with him.

'You've packed light,' I said in way of greeting.

He chuckled, and I opened the door wider so he could actually fit through it. 'Just need the bare essentials for the moment. My place isn't too far to grab stuff from.'

I spotted his car parked on the road. It stood out from the others parked down my road. His wealth stuck out like a sore thumb.

'Are you sure you don't mind parking your car there?' I asked, unable to stop myself. I hated the question. It showed something about me I wasn't proud of.

'Should I mind?' he asked, placing his bag down under my coat hooks and stepping back to bring the box in.

I shrugged. 'It's a nice car, and my road ... isn't.'

Dylan assessed me, his gaze piercing, but he chose to stay quiet.

'Okay, so I assume you know this and that you knew this when you asked to stay,' I said, trying not to ramble but letting my nerves get the better of me, 'but there's only one bedroom in this flat.'

'Yeah'—he smiled, his top lip curling upwards—'I'm aware.'

'Good, good.' My hands fidgeted, wringing together. 'Okay, so.' I looked around, not wanting to stare at him.

Why the fuck was I suddenly acting like I'd never spent time with him without other people around?

We'd literally spent every day together for the past two weeks.

'Do you want my room?' I asked, gesturing to the door at the end of the hall. Make that the only door at the end of the hall, obviously. 'Or we could share if you wanted? I promise I won't attack you.'

Geez, I needed a drink and to calm the heck down.

'I don't mind sleeping on the sofa,' he said, and my heart swooned. Literally swooned.

Then it stopped swooning and beat really fast. He'd rejected me again, hadn't he?

I needed to stop putting myself in situations where he could reject me. My mental state could really do without it.

Our eyes locked, his gaze so open and earnest that my heart returned to its former swooning, rejection completely forgotten. Well, maybe not forgotten, but put to bed. Or to sofa.

Dylan was the perfect gentleman, standing there all suave in his grey suit, looking so sexy I could die from looking at him.

Water. I needed water.

And maybe a fan.

With my flat being open plan, the moment you came through the front door into my "hallway" you were also in my living room and kitchen, too.

I turned my back on Dylan, heading straight to the counter to grab a glass and fill it up from the ice and water dispenser in my pride and joy—otherwise known as my fridge.

Having a fridge with a water and ice dispenser had been a dream of mine ever since I used the one the Winters had growing up. The moment I got my first payout from a sponsor, I put down the deposit and first year's rent on my flat and proceeded to the nearest appliance store to buy said dream fridge.

The little things in life mattered.

Or at least to me, they did.

The cold water soothed my throat, and once I'd gulped down the whole thing and then refilled it, I turned back to face Dylan, who was watching me with wry amusement.

'You okay, Mads?'

'Yep.' I nodded. 'Totally fine. Nothing to see here.'

'Hmm.' He smiled, dimples appearing in his cheeks.

Oh, for fuck's sake. A girl like me couldn't deal with dimples on top of his already distracting presence.

May as well reduce myself to a pile of ashes now, burned from his glare.

'Seriously,' Dylan said, the dimpled smile lingering. 'Don't be silly about me having your room. I can sleep on the sofa for now, and once we know how long this arrangement will be, we can make a long-term decision later down the road.'

I nodded, and the thought of him staying with me for the next year flashed through my mind. Of the two of us cooking together, watching TV together, sharing the same bathroom ...

Shit!

I hadn't thought this decision through *at all.*

When he asked to move in while at the lanes on Sunday night, it came across as the perfect solution to some of our problems.

Even Dottie, with reluctance, had admitted it was a good idea. She had tried to argue it'd be better for me to move into their home and be with all three of them, but Bonnie had intervened, spouting something I doubted she believed. I'd narrowed my eyes in Bonnie's direction, suspicious, but she smiled and told me to do as I was told. So that was that, really.

Ever since the incident, being home alone caused me to feel a little unsafe, and having Dylan around would certainly help with that.

Not to mention the eye candy potential of catching him en route to the shower.

No, that sounded pervy, and I didn't mean it like that.

Oh, I don't know. Everything was so up in the air and saying yes to him made sense at the moment.

I needed to change the subject before I imploded.

So I said, 'You ready for dinner? I'll cook.'

CHAPTER 19

madison

DYLAN'S PRESENCE, AS ALWAYS, SET MY BODY aflame.

We may've been sitting on the sofa, each on our phones, minding our own business, but regardless of that, I could sense his every action.

Dylan had a pint glass gripped in his right hand, the foam at the top of his beer bubbling and fizzing out over the top onto his tanned skin. I watched as the bubbles settled and burst.

A trusty glass of rosé clutched in my left hand, and if literally anybody else sat beside me, I'd feel at ease.

'We should put something on,' I said, breaking the silence. The blank TV loomed in front of us, and I no longer wanted to view our weird moment reflected in its darkness. 'Anything in particular you fancy watching?'

Dylan lifted his head from his phone screen and looked at the blank TV. 'You can choose.'

'None of that,' I insisted, grabbing the remote. 'There has to be something we can both agree on.'

He placed his phone down on the arm of the sofa, turning to give me his full attention.

'I'll bite,' he said. 'What have you got in mind?'

'How about the new series of *Stalker: offline*?'

He raised an eyebrow in my direction, a question on his face.

'Okay, no true crime. Got it.' I pressed the buttons on the remote until we were in a new category. 'How about *Rules of Engagement*?'

'That film Dahlia's obsessed with?' I nodded. 'No thanks. Did you know Bridger Daniels lives in Noah's block in the penthouse?'

I shook my head, filing that information away for a later date. Dahlia would wet herself if she knew that. 'Assume you've not passed that snippet on to your sister?'

He laughed. 'Think Hallie told her.' Ah, I forgot Noah's girlfriend, Hallie, was Dahlia's best friend. They co-owned the salon together and had been friends since school.

'Okay, so no period dramas either ...' I was running out of viable options. 'A-ha!' I nudged my head towards the TV. 'How about *Meet Your Match*?'

'That new dating show?'

'Yep. It's meant to be a totally new concept, never done before, which I find highly unlikely.'

'I try to avoid dating shows as a rule.'

'And you do love rules,' I blurted.

'I do,' he agreed, smiling at me. 'I don't understand all these reality dating shows. They all say they're there to find love, but we all know that's total bullshit. Maybe one out of the thirty contestants is genuine, but the others, they're all in it to make a name for themselves.'

I couldn't deny that. I'd met most of the contestants at events over the past couple of years and they'd be the first to admit the reasons they *really* took part.

'I think what I find so funny about them is how everybody is looking to find their true partner and settle down with them, and for some reason, their version of settling down always includes marriage and children. As if that's the only way you can truly be happy in your ever after.'

I'd mulled over the thought in my mind for years but had never spoken it aloud. Even Dot, the person who made me the most comfortable, who would always let me tell my truth, wouldn't understand. Her dream since childhood was to become a mum to a large brood and marry young.

Maybe my relationship with my own parents had skewed my vision of marriage and children. It had definitely skewed my idea of love.

Dylan, unaware of my racing thoughts, nodded his head with enthusiasm. 'Right! It pisses me off how society still expects that to be the goal for everybody like we're still living in the eighteenth century or some shit.'

My heart skipped a beat.

'I thought you didn't believe in love anymore.' He'd mentioned it when he told me about Caroline.

'I do,' he said. 'I ... may have told a little white lie to my friends and family so they'd stop setting me up with people.'

'Ah.'

'After everything with Caroline, it was easier to have everybody think of me as somebody who no longer believed in love or happiness.'

'Well, you've done a great job of it,' I said. 'I believed it.'

He smiled. 'I want love, eventually, but marriage has never appealed to me and neither has having kids.'

'Me either.' I smiled back, putting the remote down on the coffee table and turning to face him fully, pulling my feet up beneath my body. 'I've never met somebody who feels like that, though.'

'You're only nineteen,' Dylan said as if the sentence wasn't the most cutting thing he could have said to me. 'People expect you to change your mind.'

'And do you think that, too?'

He winced. Maybe he realised how his words sounded. 'No. I just know what other people will say, that's all.'

'When did you realise?'

'When everybody, Caroline most of all, expected me to propose on our five-year anniversary. It was the last thing I wanted, and at first, I wondered if it was because I didn't want to marry Caroline, and not because I didn't want to marry at all. But as time passed, it became clearer to me. I don't think marriage automatically means you're in a committed, loving relationship. Look at how many people get divorced.'

'Right!' The wine in my glass spilt over onto my leg when I bounced in agreement. 'And to me, loving somebody and committing yourself to the relationship is what matters. The life you build together matters. And not having children only means you can enjoy your time as a couple without the responsibilities and needs of others.'

'You a mind reader, Mads?'

I laughed. 'No. I just know what I want.'

His eyebrows raised at my certainty.

Dylan Winters was made for me, even down to his future wants, but it appeared to me I was the only one who recognised that.

'The way my parents treated me made me view the world differently than my friends. Than Dot, for example.' I took a sip of wine, savouring the taste of sweet berries before continuing. Talking about my parents made liquid courage a necessity. 'Did you know my mum tried to sell me?' I asked, my tone matter of fact. The scorn, bitter and blazing at the time, long dispersed, leaving nothingness in its wake.

Dylan, who had taken a sip of his beer, choked, trying to keep it in his mouth. 'Sorry?'

'Yeah, once my dad overdosed and finances got tighter than ever before. It was the final nail in the coffin for me to get this place.' I gestured around the minimalist setting. 'I'd have moved into a literal shoe box if it meant getting away from her.'

'They never deserved to have a daughter as loving and caring as you.' Dylan shook his head, anger lingering in his eyes. 'Mum and Dad would talk about you and them when us kids were in bed, and they'd get so mad. I've never understood how your own parents could be so blind to how great you are.'

Tears welled in my eyes. Hearing the words from Dylan made them mean more than if they'd come from anybody else.

'You don't have contact with her anymore, right?' Dylan asked, and I shook my head in response. 'Well, while we're on the topic of honesty ...' Dylan placed his glass down on the coffee table. 'I'd be lying if I said I wasn't relieved when Caroline cheated on me.'

That wasn't what I'd expected him to say.

At all.

'Colour me intrigued, Mr Winters.'

'As you know, the two of us met at university, and I suppose it seemed inevitable we'd become a couple. We both had similar interests and enjoyed spending time together. But as time went by, it became clear to me that Caroline had … exaggerated how much we had in common. She wanted to be a trophy wife with a top lawyer husband and two kids whom she dressed nicely and showed off on social media. Which, as you now know, is the last thing I wanted. So I pulled back. Worked more. Anything to avoid the awful scenes she'd make, begging to know why I hadn't yet proposed. All intimacy between us ended, and I was relieved because it meant she couldn't get pregnant and force us into a life I increasingly didn't want.'

I waited, sensing it was the first time he'd let it all out.

'Then she slept with one of my mates from school.' He chuckled. 'That makes it sound like she only did it once, but in actuality, it went on behind my back for months.'

'Ouch.'

'I'm over it. God, I was over it pretty much the moment it happened. My pride hurt more than anything else, but the fact it didn't hurt more than that told me all I needed to know. So when she apologised and begged for forgiveness, it was kinder to let it go. Stop the farce.'

I leaned forwards, reaching for my wineglass with both hands and sat back, taking a thoughtful sip.

'I can't imagine having the gall to cheat on somebody for months and then beg for forgiveness like nothing happened.'

'That's because you're nothing like Caroline, Mads. You

have a huge heart, and you care about people. Even when Dottie's being the biggest brat known to man, you still care about her; love her.' He swallowed, his eyes looking into mine, and all I wanted to do was drown in them. 'You deserve the best in this life, Madison.'

dylan

CREDITS SCROLLED ACROSS THE SCREEN, AND Madison yawned.

'Well, that's a sign it's time for bed,' I said. 'Same time tomorrow night?'

After our deep conversation, we picked the first episode in a mystery thriller series and settled down in silence to watch it unfold.

'But I want to know what happens to the dog,' Madison said, fighting through another yawn.

'The fate of the dog won't change before tomorrow night.' I stood, reaching out my hand to help her up. 'Plus, it draws out the tension if I make you wait.'

The double meaning of my words wasn't lost on me, but once said, words couldn't be stuffed back in.

Madison took my hand, and I pulled her up to stand chest-to-chest with me.

Yet another mark against me and my poor decisions.

Why on earth was I going out of my way to put myself in bad situations with her?

I could want her, sure, but I couldn't act on it!

That path only led nowhere good.

Madison laughed. 'Because what the two of us need is more tension.'

The pain that shot through me when I laughed back took me by surprise. *What the?*

My lower back throbbed with pain, the slightest movement aggravating whatever was going on in there.

Madison stepped back. 'Are you okay?'

'It's like I turned thirty and my body's turned into a glow stick, cracks galore.'

'Are you sure you're okay on the lumpy sofa?' Madison asked, worry in her gaze. 'Using some of earlier's honesty, the sofa is super old. I got it from a charity shop when I moved into this place and never got around to replacing it. It's seen better days, that's for sure.'

'It's all good.' My smile, more of a grimace, did little to convince her.

'Are you sure? Because I can swap with you. It's not a problem.'

'Don't be silly. This is your place.'

'That you're only staying in because of me.' She stood on her tiptoes and tilted my head down so we were looking at one another. 'Please, Dill. Don't make me feel even more guilty than I already do.'

I didn't want her to feel guilty, but I also didn't want her to deal with the lumpy sofa either. The two nights I'd already spent on it were no doubt the reason my back had decided to give up on me, but I didn't want her to know that.

'Okay, if you're not gonna let me take the sofa,' she said,

her eyes burning with determination, 'then come share my bed with me.'

'I—'

'I'm not gonna take no for an answer, Dylan.'

She stamped her foot, which broke the spell of our interlocked eyes and the rising tension. I looked down at her foot, then back to her face, one eyebrow raised in question.

'Did you just stamp your foot at me?'

She folded her arms across her chest in defiance. 'So what if I did? What you gonna do about it?'

'I'm going to—' I reached forwards to tickle her or surprise her, or, who knew really, but what ended up happening was me crying out in pain because my back sent a lightning bolt through me.

Maybe it was time to admit defeat—in more ways than one.

'Fine,' I bit out, hating the taste of it. 'We can share your bed.'

IF YOU'D TOLD me a month ago, I would be sharing a bed with Madison Jones, well, I would never have believed you.

Mainly because I hadn't seen her in years at that point, but also a huge factor being she was my younger sister's best friend and had been since literal primary school. Not to mention Dottie's made it clear multiple times her friends were off-limits.

Watching her move around her bedroom was surreal.

She grabbed some sleep clothes, plus some other bits, before heading out into the hall. 'I won't be long.'

I nodded, unable to speak, and she left with a small smile playing on her lips.

She returned, and I went off to the bathroom to sort myself out and brush my teeth.

When did life get so complicated?

By the time I got back to Madison's room, she lay in her king-size bed on the right-hand side, scrolling through her phone.

'Have you found it hard?' I blurted out.

She startled. 'What?'

'Have you found it hard?' I repeated, then clarified. 'Not posting online?'

Her face turned thoughtful, and I used her distraction to get into bed without having to look at her.

There I was, a grown man getting in bed with the girl I wanted more than anything, yet I couldn't act on it. It's time I finally accepted how much she'd grown on me. Every time she entered a room, it lit up. Every time she turned her megawatt smile my way, my insides fluttered. Fucking fluttered.

Life was cruel.

'No,' she finally replied. 'It's been quite nice not having to be so *on* all the time, ya know? Like I can be my real self without worrying what somebody will think or how they'll perceive me.'

'I can imagine it gets exhausting having to always be aware of what others think.'

'It does, truly.' She sighed, putting her phone down on the bedside cabinet to her left before getting comfortable. 'Honestly, I'm not sure if I want to go back to it. At least, not in the same way.'

'What would you rather do?' I plumped the pillow and rested my head, gazing up at the ceiling, trying to stop myself from thinking of how close we were.

'I'd love to start a YouTube channel,' she said, her tone wistful. 'Do my make-up while talking about topics interesting to me. Commentary, maybe, or crime. I don't know. Something like that anyway.' She laughed. I could differentiate her laughs—knew their meanings—and she was embarrassed.

'I think you'd do great,' I said. 'People would subscribe, no doubt about it.'

The bed moved with the shake of her head.

'I don't know. People have me down as an airhead with nothing important to say.'

'Do they? Or is that how you view yourself?'

'I—' Madison paused, both speaking and moving. 'I guess I've never thought of it like that before.'

She shuffled into a different position, as did I, neither of us wanting to touch the other by accident.

Maybe it wasn't too late to go back to the sofa.

'Night, Dill,' she said, flicking the light switch on her bedside lamp.

'Night, Mads,' I whispered, doing the same, washing us in darkness.

dylan

MADISON AND MY SISTERS WERE HAVING A GIRLS' day, meaning absolutely no older brothers allowed, so that left me with little to do except wait around until they needed a lift home.

When Noah asked me if I wanted to meet him at the gym, I jumped on it. Since the murder and spending all my spare time with Madison, I'd barely got to look at him, let alone talk to him about anything real.

'Come on,' Noah said, looking up at me from the bench. 'Tell Uncle Noah everything.'

'Not much to tell.'

'Let's not start the day off with a lie, ay?' Noah stood, wiping his face with his towel. 'We've been mates long enough for me to know when you've got something on your mind. So come on. Spill.'

'The truth?' Noah nodded, waiting. 'I'm fucked, mate.'

'What did you do?'

'Nothing ... yet, but that's a part of the problem.'

'You sort of need to explain what you mean ...'

'Basically, ever since Wednesday night, the two of us have shared her bed because the sofa nearly threw my back out.' I rubbed my jaw, attempting to collect my thoughts before spewing them into the universe. 'And even though we fall asleep with inches of space between us, every single morning, we've woken up with her wrapped around me like a rash.'

'Ah,' Noah said, 'that sounds complicated.'

'It is. Especially as I've realised, I *like her* like her.'

'How about you just tell the girl you want to see how it goes between you?' Noah's raised eyebrows told me all I needed about his opinion of it all. 'You're both punishing yourselves, and for what?'

'For starters, it'd look poor jobwise. Jeoff and Mick made it clear I had to keep it in my trousers around her. Our case would be thrown right out if anybody caught wind I wanted to bang our lead witness.'

'And?' Noah prompted, his smile wide, and totally punchable.

'*And,*' I sputtered, pissed that Noah continued to push me. 'There's my family to think about. Dottie to think about.'

'Dottie's a grown adult. She'll get over it.'

'But will she though?' I shook my head. 'You forget, Dot believes she has a claim on Madison, or at least she believes she does. She treats her like a possession. Her favourite toy.'

'Yeah, I'm not hearing anything new that'd make me tell you to back off. If anything, your sister could do with being shown life isn't fair, and you can't treat people like you own them.'

He had a fair point, but who wanted to have that battle with Dottie? Not me.

I shivered at the mere thought of it.

'Have you met Dottie?'

'I have, and I know she's your sister, mate, but she's a spoiled brat.'

I nodded in agreement. 'Enough about me.' I grabbed my towel and walked over to the hallway that led to the changing rooms. 'How's things going for you?'

'Yeah, yeah, all good, thanks. The new sign at the office is going up within the week, so that's pretty exciting. Means a lot more meetings, though.'

The new signage for Taylor, Roberts & James would make his partnership official, and honestly, nobody deserved it more than Noah.

Noah continued talking, but my mind went to Madison.

I hoped she was having a good time, getting to relax with the others. Her whole life had been upended since she witnessed what she did, and it worried me whenever she went quiet, in case she was reliving it in her mind.

She deserved a relaxing day.

Fuck, she deserved everything she went after.

I hoped she didn't spill anything that could make things awkward for us, like how the two of us were sharing her bed, waking up entangled, then never mentioning it afterwards.

I had faith in her.

Mads wouldn't want any unnecessary attention.

madison

CARILLO'S, THE BEST BURGER PLACE IN THE CITY, was filled with a lively energy.

Bottomless brunch was well underway, and already I had no idea how many cocktails I'd consumed.

And like the alcohol, gossip was a-flowing.

'Isaac Wilson is the most irritating man I've ever met!' Dana said, seething. 'He's the new librarian I mentioned the other week.' She nudged her head in Dahlia's direction, who nodded back. 'He's shown up out of literal nowhere. Moved to Lakeland because he wanted to leave the city behind or some such shit. And I can't stand him!'

Dana, the most laid-back, calm woman in existence, had become a raging ball of fire at the mere mention of him.

It surprised me how livid she looked, continuing to talk while I flagged down a server to come and take our order for another round.

The beauty of a bottomless brunch at Carillo's was that they really meant bottomless—plus, they included the good cocktails, unlike the places that only let you have prosecco or a pornstar martini at an extra cost.

'... and then the stupid bastard goes and tells me I've put a whole trolley of books back in the wrong place,' Dana said, the large glass in her hand threatening to spill over as she gestured while telling her story. 'Me! Coming from a guy who doesn't even know the Dewey Decimal system by heart!'

Dana stopped to take a deep breath—and a large gulp of her drink.

'But that's enough about me. If I keep talking about him, we'll never talk about anything else.'

The server I'd flagged over finally arrived and took our round, hurrying off to get them made.

The art of bottomless brunch, something we'd all perfected, was that you should never have an empty glass in front of you. The moment your drink reached half-full, you could order another, and we took every advantage of that rule.

'Mads,' Dahlia said, focusing everyone's attention in my direction. 'You've been awfully quiet today.'

'Well,' I said with a laugh, tilting my glass Dana's way. 'I'd much rather listen to Dana's irritation at Isaac than bore you all with my shit.'

'You look pretty tired actually,' Dottie said. The girl had never learned tact in her life. 'Are you not getting much sleep with everything going on?'

I jumped on the excuse she'd unknowingly given me. 'It's hard to relax, to be honest. And every time I close my eyes, I see ...' I trailed off, letting them envision the worst.

But if I was being honest, what I'd witnessed had fuck all to do with how little sleep I was getting.

Nope.

The true reason? My proximity to Dylan every night and being unable to act on my feelings towards him.

I kept expecting him to back away, or move back to the sofa, or at least mention the fact we keep waking up wrapped in one another's bodies, but nada.

If anything, he went out of his way to avoid the subject entirely.

'Well,' Dottie said, breaking through my brain fog. 'At least you've got Dylan asleep on your sofa to keep you safe.'

My eyes shifted away from the table.

Must look anywhere but at their concerned faces.

Dahlia's eye caught mine for a brief second, but then her suspicious look disappeared as quickly as it had arrived.

'Well, how are things going with you?' I asked Dottie, throwing the attention her way. Something she usually loved.

'What about me?' she asked, her tone brittle and nowhere near its usual chirpy self.

'How are things going with Braydon?'

'Braydon's history,' Dottie said dully.

'Oh,' was all I could think to say.

We all took sips of our drinks, and I once more flagged down the server, and mouthed 'same again'.

He nodded, and I looked back at the group.

'What's going on with you?' Dottie asked Dahlia. 'I feel like I barely get to spend time with you, and I live with you!'

'Things have been super busy at the salon. Nothing to report here, friends.'

The next round of drinks arrived.

As much as I wanted to keep drinking, I was also super aware of how uninhibited alcohol made me, and I didn't want to slip up and say something about Dylan.

Instead of gulping down half the glass so I could order another round, I took a small, dainty sip.

Dahlia's assessing gaze met mine.

The look said: *you're hiding things from me, and I'm going to find out what.*

madison

DYLAN, EVER THE GOOD BROTHER, PICKED ME AND his sisters up from Carillo's and drove them to their respective homes.

By the time brunch finished, they were all pretty drunk —me not too far behind them, even after deciding to limit myself.

Dylan threw himself down on the sofa. 'Well, it looks like you girls had a good day.'

I laughed. 'We did. Even if most of the conversation revolved around Dana and her new nemesis.'

Once we'd piled into the car, Dana had filled Dylan in on her hatred of Isaac. Pretty sure everybody in the restaurant knew about it by the time we departed.

Her dislike loud and hard to ignore.

'What has he even done to irk her so much?'

'You mean other than showing up?' I laughed more. 'She mentioned he didn't know the Dewey Decimal system by heart, which, as I'm sure you can imagine, is blasphemous to Dana.'

I took my spot beside Dylan, keeping a gap between our bodies.

'Dana looked fit to burst while telling us about him. Isaac should watch his back, that's all I'm saying.'

'It's always the quieter ones who have a flair for the dramatic.'

'Dana's always been dramatic,' I pointed out. 'She's just always overshadowed by Dottie, so it's less noticeable.'

'Very true.' Dylan turned the TV on and instantly got up the next episode of the series we were making our way through. 'You think he'll push her too far and one day she'll explode?'

'Oh, clear enemies-to-lovers vibes are coming off that whole situation!' I said. 'I wonder how long it'll take for them to realise it.'

'Anything else said for me to know about?'

I shook my head. 'Nope. Dahlia said she had nothing to report. Oh! Dottie said Braydon's history, which let's be honest, we all knew from the moment we met him.' Dylan hummed his agreement. 'They mentioned I look tired.'

'Yeah?'

'Yeah. Dottie said how it's a good thing I've got you sleeping on the sofa to protect me. Didn't think it wise to correct her.'

'I should move back to the sofa.'

'Don't be silly.' I waved him off. Of course he'd say something like that. The alcohol lingering in my system had me opening my mouth. 'Maybe if the two of us spoke properly and got our heads out of our arses, we'd be able to get a good night's sleep.'

'Did you just tell me I need to get my head out of my arse?'

'Technically, I said it about myself, too.'

'Right.' Dylan plumped the cushion behind him, rested back on it, and then leaned forwards again to re-plump it. I watched him like a creep, waiting for him to keep talking.

His fight with the cushion was apparently more important.

Every time he put it into a position he was happy with, the cushion sagged back down in an instant.

'Maybe we should get a new sofa,' Dylan said, accepting defeat, resting back once more.

I liked the *we*.

'We could go tomorrow if you're free?' I said, tone hopeful.

'Sounds good to me. So what were you saying? Heads and arses?'

I laughed. 'What I mean is maybe we should talk honestly and put it all on the table.'

'Well, seeing as this is your brilliant idea, you can go first.'

I took a deep breath. 'Okay ...' Where to start? Maybe it was best to dive in and go for it. 'So every morning, we wake up tangled together and then say nothing about it, get up, and go about our day as if it means nothing.'

'It means nothing.'

'Way to hurt my ego, Dill.' Jeez, the man could gut me like a fish with one sentence, yet I stood tall—or rather sat tall. 'What I mean,' I emphasised, 'is that I quite like waking up with your heartbeat under my palm. It doesn't mean I want to jump you.'

Cough, cough, lie, lie.

'If we accept that we're gonna touch in our sleep, then maybe we'll both get better rest, no longer worrying about an accidental leg graze or hand hold or whatever.'

Dylan looked at me as if he were seeing me, *truly seeing me,* for the first time.

A wide smile I couldn't contain broke out on my face.

I quite enjoyed surprising him.

'We're both adults,' I said with a finality he couldn't argue with. 'So let's act like it.'

madison

Our new sofa took up a lot more space in the living room than my previous one, but man, it made the place look a whole lot better.

It hadn't taken us long to pick it out. Pretty much from the moment we walked into the furniture showroom, we fell in love with it.

We'd picked out a rigid sofa in the Chesterfield style. All dark-green velvet with space for two people to sit comfortably, but absolutely impractical for anybody to sleep on.

I bloody loved it.

Dylan had gone to the office early, and for the first time since the murder, he allowed me to stay home alone.

The office, while having super friendly staff and a gorgeous-looking Dylan, had little else to occupy my time. There was only so much I could gossip with Dawn about the goings-on of the people who worked there.

It had taken a while to get Dylan to agree to leave me at home, but I told him I'd go and visit Bonnie at the lanes once I finished all the housework that had gone undone.

Never realised how many clothes I had to wash until I stopped having the time.

I dusted the windowsills, the easiest of the tasks on my to-do list, and took notice of the goings on outside. I loved looking at my street and seeing what people were getting up to. It was a fun way to pass the time.

Doris, two doors down, always had her shopping delivered on a Thursday.

Mark, at number twenty-five, liked clean windows, and you'd often spot him up on a ladder cleaning away. I'd asked him once why he didn't hire a company to do it for him. *'Because no bugger but me can work to my satisfaction.'*

Mark made me laugh.

As I dusted, I looked out and spotted a car I'd never seen before parked directly outside my place. Not surprising. There were so many people living on my street, and so many households with multiple cars these days, that it was rare to recognise every car. But the person inside the car made me pause.

He was bald, in his mid-sixties, and smoking a cigarette out the half-opened driver window.

Staring straight at me.

Shit.

A shiver travelled down my spine, but I pulled my gaze away. Of course he wasn't looking *at* me, just in the direction of my place. Probably waiting for somebody or some other perfectly good explanation.

I continued with my cleaning, forcing myself to keep my eyes away from the window.

My paranoia had definitely crept up a few notches,

which made total sense seeing as I witnessed some guy stabbing another.

Hours passed.

As I hoovered the living room, I spotted the man again, standing on the corner of my front path. He was no longer looking towards my place, though, but at something in the distance, out of view.

People were walking by the man, but none of them were interacting.

Of course people were walking by.

Yes, I was acting paranoid and suspicious and anxious and all the things, but I couldn't help the what if from living in the dark recesses of my brain.

Should I call Dylan? No. No need to disturb him at work for no reason. Not like anything had happened. I was acting silly.

Extremely heightened imagination. My teachers had said that about me growing up more times than I could count.

I closed the blinds. Maybe that would help take my mind away from it all.

A knock came at my front door.

My breathing picked up its pace, my heart beating a mile a minute.

On light toes, I walked to the door to look through the peephole.

The bald man from the car stood there, raising his clenched fist to knock again.

A bad feeling washed over me. Something wasn't right.

In fact, something was *very, very* wrong.

Without thinking twice, I rushed to my bedroom at the

end of the hall, knowing nobody could look in on me there. I closed the blinds anyway, just in case.

My phone was in my hand in seconds.

The call to Dylan connected straight away.

'Mads, everything okay?'

His voice down the line soothed me, and the moment he asked if everything was okay, I started sobbing.

'Mads, what's going on? Talk to me.' Dylan's distress at my distress only had me crying harder.

'Please come home,' I begged, fighting through my tears. 'I need you.'

dylan

MICK CALLED AN IMPORTANT MEETING THE moment I entered the building after my lunch break.

'What's going on?' I asked Noah, waiting at the drinks station for me, a cup of black coffee already made for me in his hand.

He shrugged. 'Good and bad news is all I can make out from the little Mick told me. Jeoff's not here, though. Another case has landed in his lap, and we can't pass it up. Some big rock star is being accused of murder.'

'Yeah, can't turn that kind of publicity down.'

We made our way into the meeting room and took our seats as the others all filed in, each with a large mug in their hands and a brittle smile on their faces.

Mick swaggered in not long after.

'Wonderful, you're all here already. Okay, let's keep this brief, as I know we've all got a lot to be getting on with.'

He looked at us all, stopping at the head of the desk.

'Okay, starting with the good news. They found Malcolm Silver late last night up north. They've arrested and charged him with the murder of Toby Scott, meaning our case against him is moving ahead. The case against Lawrence will unfold once Malcolm admits it was him who hired him.'

Everybody murmured their excitement. Good news indeed.

'Now for the bad news.' Mick winced, his eyes finding me. 'Somehow, The Syndicate's aware we have a witness. Malcolm said as much during questioning. We are currently uncertain whether they know her identity.'

My phone buzzed in my pocket. An incoming call.

From Madison.

I stood and left the room, indicating to Mick I had to take the call.

There was no reason for her to call me. Honestly, I hadn't expected her to, seeing as she hadn't had time to herself in a while and probably had a lot of things to catch up on.

I answered the phone. 'Mads, everything okay?'

Sobbing made its way to my ear, and my heart lurched.

'Mads, what's going on?' I looked through the unfogged glass window to Noah and shrugged at his head tilted in question. 'Talk to me.'

'Please come home.' Her voice was broken. 'I need you.'

'What's happened?' I went straight to the door that led out of the office and to the lift, pressing hard on the down button to call it to me.

'A m-man's been watching my place for hours, and now he's knocking on the d-door.' Her sobs broke me.

'Mads, stay where you are, okay? I'll be home as soon as I can.'

And although it may not be the right time to think

about it, my words rang true to me. In a short time, her place had become the place I called home.

———

THE ENTIRE DRIVE HOME, Madison's sobbing replayed in my head.

Over and over.

A sickening loop, never ending.

I hadn't even told anybody before I bolted.

Noah would understand and no doubt make some kind of excuse for me. Or maybe Mick would realise I'd left to check on Madison. If The Syndicate did, in fact, know about her, then she was in even more danger.

The person at her door could link to the case, and I wasn't about to leave her at home, alone, in tears, for longer than necessary.

All her life, Madison faced adversity, strong and resilient, never letting the downs get to her.

But the terror in her voice gutted me, a sound unfamiliar.

I parked my car at an angle, too preoccupied with getting home, and went straight to the front door.

Nobody stood outside, and when I stopped to survey the street, everything looked to be in its place. No glaring discrepancies or anything like that.

Doris waved at me from where she pottered around with her plants.

'Everything okay, Dylan?' she called.

Maybe she'd seen something.

'Doris,' I said, walking over so I didn't have to shout at

her. 'Did you see someone at Madison's door earlier today? A man?'

Doris shook her blue-rinsed head. 'No, dear. Road's mostly been quiet today. The odd passer-by of course, but nothing too odd.'

'If you see anything, would you mind passing it along? I'd appreciate it if you did.'

'Of course, dear.' She patted my hand, her skin like soft leather. 'I'm so glad Madison's got a wonderful partner like you to look out for her these days.'

I didn't correct her assumption, but instead said, 'Thank you, Doris. I'll speak to you later.'

I jogged to Madison's door and let myself in with my key.

'Mads?' I called out, closing the door behind me. 'It's me.'

I couldn't find her in the living room or the kitchen; my eyes glossed over the new sofa we picked out together the day before, and I smiled at the memory.

A whimper came from Madison's bedroom.

The sight of her on the floor in the foetal position had my heart tearing in two. Shaking, scared witless. It killed me. Madison should never be so sad. So broken.

'I'm here,' I whispered, reaching out to touch her. To soothe her.

I lay on the floor behind her, my arm draped across her hip.

'Everything's going to be okay.' My heart thudded in my chest. 'From now on, unless you're with one of my family, you're not leaving my sight. You're mine to protect until this is over, okay?'

I breathed in her scent. Pressed my lips to the back of her head.

'I've got you,' I whispered, pulling her as close to me as I could without hurting her. 'I'll keep you safe, no matter what.'

madison

I WAVED GOODBYE TO BONNIE AS SHE DROVE AWAY before closing the door behind me in relief. I found socialising hard enough without having to avoid a ton of questions you couldn't answer.

Bonnie meant well, though.

Like a mother hen, she'd taken me under her wing all day. Made sure I wanted for nothing, that I was safe, fed, and happy.

Something I'd never experienced with my own mother.

Once alone, everything from the day before rushed at me. Since Dylan had dropped me off in the morning at the lanes to spend the day with Bonnie, I'd barely had time to think it all over.

After Dylan had come home and found me crying, he lay behind me, hugging me to his warm chest for an hour before coaxing me to eat some dinner and watch TV with him.

He truly was the perfect gentleman.

A perfect gentleman who messaged me not too long ago to say he'd arrive home a few minutes after me.

Home.

He called it home.

A knock came at the door, and I opened it, fully expecting Dylan to be standing on the other side.

If I'd even paused for a moment, I wouldn't have opened it. Especially not after the events of the day before. But I didn't stop and think, too excited at the thought of seeing Dylan again. It slipped my mind completely that he had a key now and wouldn't need to knock.

My mother, Jessa James, stood in the doorway instead, looking a hell of a lot worse than the last time I had the misfortune of being in her presence, which was saying something.

'Madison,' she said, her rasping voice one from my nightmares. 'Nice to see you.'

'Wish I could say the same.' I took a deep breath to calm myself down. 'What are you doing here, Mum?'

What I meant: how the fuck did you find me?

Guess her sudden appearance explained the man the day before. She must have sent one of her lackeys to find me, to make sure she didn't darken the wrong doorway and all that.

Her brown hair hung lank and limp, greasy at the scalp, resembling strings of spaghetti. Her thin frame was somehow even slimmer, no meat on her bones, and her clothes at least three sizes too big for her. Probably couldn't afford new ones. No spare money to be had when you spent every penny you got on alcohol and drugs.

'Nothing wrong with a mother wanting to spend time with their daughter, is there?' She cracked a smile, revealing a cracked front tooth. 'It's been so long since we were together, Son.'

The nickname, long pushed back and repressed, rushed to the forefront of my mind. It reminded me of my dad. His favourite joke. Something funny to say again and again. I never laughed.

Your name is Madi-SON, get it? I always wanted a son, but instead, I got you, you piece of shit. So, Son it is.

It amazed me how much a memory could affect you, even long after the person in it had died, making the world a better place without them in it.

Mum continued talking. 'Not gonna invite your dear old mother inside?' She nudged her head towards my flat, but I kept the door firmly in the grip of my left hand. No foot of hers would get inside. I wouldn't allow it.

'No,' I said, narrowing my gaze. 'I'm gonna ask again, and you're going to answer truthfully this time, and then you're going to leave, never to return. What are you doing here?'

The surprise in her eyes thrilled me. I'd never spoken to her with such conviction before. Never stood my ground.

I was no longer the same girl who'd left her home eighteen months ago.

'I need money.'

I laughed. 'Of course you do.'

She had no other reason for her to seek me out, to come to find me. She'd never done it before, so it made sense the only reason she had was because her money issues had got worse.

'You're a useless daughter, you know that? Never helped me, even when you came into all your money. No, you were more than happy to let me starve. Live in filth. Drown in debt.'

A lead weight kept my tongue down, preventing me from snapping back.

'I know you've made good money posting your shit online, but it was only the other month when I read the articles about Dottie's birthday party it hit me how much you must be making.' Mum shook her head, the hatred on her face ever-present. 'And yet you've left me out in the cold. Left me to suffer.' Her spit landed on my face. 'You disgust me.'

'If I disgust you that much, then why do you want my money? Oh wait, it's because you've spunked yours away like you always do.' I laughed, bitterness rising within me. 'You're a shit mum, and I deserve a lot better than you.'

'Like that cow, Bonnie Winters?' she snapped. 'I watched her drop you off here just now.'

'Bonnie's a true mother. She cares about me.' My voice lost its fight, ready to have her gone and out of my life once more.

Dylan couldn't come home and find her at our door. I needed to get rid of her.

'Mum, you've asked what you wanted, and I've given you my answer. Now leave me alone. And don't come back.'

I slammed the door in her face.

dylan

THE LAST PERSON I EXPECTED AT OUR FRONT DOOR when I returned from work was Jessa James.

Madison's mother, if you could even call her that, always filled me with an inexplicable amount of rage. Probably had to do with the fact that she was a terrible person and an abusive parent.

I couldn't interrupt their argument. Madison would never forgive me if I burst in and attempted to act the saviour. Plus, from where I stood, she seemed to be handling herself more than fine.

I'd had to park my car around the corner, and Madison hadn't spotted me yet, so I waited it out a bit.

Madison's voice floated over. 'Mum, you've asked what you wanted, and I've given you my answer. Now leave me alone. And don't come back.'

The front door slammed in Jessa's face, and I bit down my chuckle.

Jessa waited a moment before turning around and

stomping her way down the path like a kid who didn't get their way.

She looked awful.

Obviously, Madison had told me a bit about her, and I had my own memories of her from years gone by, but it had been a while since I'd physically seen her.

Her sunken face, her bloodshot beady eyes, and her thin frame would make me pity her if I knew nothing about her as a person.

I stayed hidden until she'd stormed off in the opposite direction.

Then, after another minute, I made my way up the path to the front door.

I let myself in and found Madison hovering over by the kitchen counter, her back to me.

'Hey,' I said. 'Everything okay?'

'Hey,' she replied, spinning on the spot to face me, her trusty glass of water gripped in her hand. 'I'm good. How was your day?'

'Same old, honestly. Dawn sends her love.'

'That woman is a sweetheart. Oh! I meant to tell you. She said she'll bring in some fudge for us on Friday. It's her speciality.'

'Her fudge is to die for.' I nodded, reaching above Madison's head to grab a glass from the cupboard, my arm grazing her body as I did it. 'Anything exciting happened in your day to tell me about?'

I nudged her, wanting her to open up and tell me about her mum's visit, but she didn't bite.

'After you dropped me at the lanes, I worked behind the

shoe counter for a bit. Didn't realise how much I missed the smell of the aerosol cleaning spray. It brings back so many happy memories, you know?'

I nodded. The smell of that spray would forever be imprinted on the insides of my nostrils.

'And then me and your mum had lunch while your dad and Jimmy took over.'

I made myself a drink and took a step back from her, needing to put myself outside of her scent bubble before I did something stupid like reach out and touch her face, my fingertips grazing softly across her cheek.

'Jimmy feels like part of the furniture he's worked at the lanes for so long. Dad would be lost without him.'

'He really would,' Mads agreed. 'After that, we were back to work. I'd forgotten how nice it could be. I miss hanging out at the lanes all the time.'

'Out of all us kids, you and Dottie definitely spent the most time there.'

'Probably because we're the youngest. You guys grew up and moved on, choosing to hang out at the cinema or the park instead.'

'I'll have you know the park can be rather cool.'

'It's where I met Dottie, back in the day.' Madison shifted her weight and smiled. 'My mum took me there and ditched me because she needed to meet a *friend* a couple of streets over. So there I sat, swinging all by myself, minding my own business, when this loud girl ran over to me.'

'Dottie is rather loud.'

'She's obnoxious. Told me I shouldn't be swinging alone.' Mads shook her head, deep in thought. 'And instead of asking if I wanted to play with her, she demanded it.'

'Sounds like our Dot.'

'Well, as we both know, whatever she says goes, so I played with her, and after that, we became best friends in the way kids do.' She took a sip of her drink. 'And even though I'm a year older and was in a different school year, it never mattered. Dottie's my one constant. The person who's always stuck around and never left me.'

A twinge, small yet defined, panged my heartstrings. To hear Mads talk so openly about her friendship with Dot, to know how she viewed it all, hurt. For years we could all see a strong bond existed between the two of them, but I supposed I never stopped to think about the *how* of its existence.

It killed me to think of Madison hurting, and a hatred so strong it burned rushed through me at the thought of all those who'd wronged her. Who had made her believe she didn't deserve love to the point where my sister's love was that important to her?

Madison whispered, breaking the silence we'd fallen into. 'Nobody's ever cared about me the way Dottie does.'

'That's not true,' I murmured. 'I care about you.'

'You care for me the way people care for their plants.'

'And how do people care for their plants?'

'They care for them too much and kill them, or they care for them in stops and starts and kill them. Either way, the plants end up dead.'

'And which one are you implying I am?'

'Does it even matter?'

I wanted to tell her about my recent realisations. That I liked her, cared for her, and wished I could allow something to happen between us.

But the words wouldn't come.

And I ruined everything, the way I had multiple times before, and said, 'You know you're a sister to me, Mads.'

madison

'*You know you're a sister to me, Mads.*'

Dylan's words from the previous evening, said with such genuine care, continued to cut me every time they ran through my head.

So basically, every minute, seeing as they existed on a loop, constantly revolving.

Even getting my hair done hadn't taken away the image of his face, the honesty in his eyes, as he said the single worst sentence he'd ever said to me.

And trust me, the sentence had plenty of competition.

In the silver-framed mirror in front of me, I watched Dahlia dye my hair, ensuring she covered every strand before moving on to the next section.

I loved having Dahlia do my hair.

It took me back to my childhood, to the days I escaped my home and went to the Winters' place instead. A place filled with love and happiness and everything my place lacked.

'Noah mentioned you're at the office all the time now,'

Hallie said from her position behind Lola, the woman in the chair next to me. 'Says Dawn will be gutted when you have to go.'

'Dawn is a total babe,' I said, a smile breaking out on my face. 'She said she'll bring fudge tomorrow.'

'Jealous!' Hallie said with enthusiasm. 'Maybe you could sneak some to Noah for me.'

I laughed. 'I'll see what I can do.'

'Isn't it good my Hallie is so happy?' Lola said. The older woman sat with one leg crossed over the other, yet somehow made it look regal. 'One of the best things I ever did, setting her up with Noah.'

'I helped,' Dahlia said, not wanting her role in the match to be forgotten. 'Maybe we should start a matchmaking service, Lola.'

'Talking about matchmaking,' Hallie said, picking up the straighteners to use on Lola's short hair. 'I've got a friend I think you'd be perfect for, Madison.'

'Me?' I said, surprised to be dragged into their talk of matchmaking. 'What about me?'

'I've got a mate who I think you'd hit it off with!' Hallie said, styling Lola's hair into spikes. She hadn't wanted to style it that way, but Lola insisted. What Lola wanted, she got. Every time.

'Oh, I'm not sure ...'

Hallie continued, ignoring the start of what would no doubt be a protest. 'When I mentioned it to Dahlia, she insisted we convince you.'

I turned an accusing gaze Dahlia's way in the mirror. She didn't bat an eye, instead choosing to smile serenely back at me.

'Go on the date, Madison!' Dahlia said with a wide smile. She was egging me on, and she knew it, too. The cow.

'I'll think about it,' I said. An answer that everybody knew meant, *I'll pretend to think about it and then say no when you ask again at a later date.*

The main reason—okay, the *only* reason—I considered saying yes was that maybe, just maybe, it would make Dylan jealous. Or at least show him that other people desired me, and I wasn't a ten-year-old kid sister anymore.

The date could go one of two ways.

It could go well. I'd have an enjoyable, nice time, and Dylan wouldn't care.

Or Dylan would care when he found out about it, and whether the date went well or not, I'd know not to let my determination towards having him die.

'His name is Jason, and he's a regular guy. Nothing like the guys you hang around with at events and that.' Hallie kept talking, unaware of my inner turmoil.

'Maybe it'll give Dylan the kick up the arse he needs,' Dahlia muttered.

'Sorry, what did you say?' I asked, unsure if I heard her correctly. Edie had turned on the water in the shampoo station, and the sound of the running shower overpowered everything else.

'I said if he hurts you, Dylan will give him a kick up the arse.'

Hmm ... I didn't question her further, but something in my gut told me she'd lied to me.

'Okay, fine.' I threw my hands up in the air, a gesture of acquiescence if there ever was one. 'I'll go on the date. What harm could it do?'

dylan

FOR THE THIRD DAY IN A ROW, I WAS IN MY OFFICE alone without Madison. I was a big enough person to admit that the lack of her presence bothered me.

It made work better, having her close by. She gave my day a relief I hadn't spotted was missing before.

But it also helped to know she was safe, and at Dahlia's salon, she would be. My sister would message me the moment something happened—if something happened.

A knock came at my door.

'Come in,' I called out, expecting it to be Mick or Jeoffrey.

Noah walked in, a large brown thin envelope in his hand, waving it around with nonchalance.

'This came for you.'

I recognised it immediately. 'Thanks.' I took it from Noah's grip and placed it on my desk as if I wasn't itching to rip it open and read the contents straight away.

Noah raised an eyebrow my way, but I turned my back on him and pretended to tidy my desk.

'Catch up tomorrow morning?' he asked.

'Sure.' I turned around again to give him a tilt of the head.

Leave. That was the word on the tip of my tongue, begging to break free.

But I kept my cool. Kind of.

With one last penetrating look, Noah left my office, closing the door with a gentle click behind him.

My fingers twitched. The need to open the envelope overriding any other work I intended to get on with.

It couldn't be put off.

I ripped the edge of the envelope, unveiling the expected typed letter inside.

> Dylan,
> Can you feel it? My breath on your neck.
> Close enough to reach out and touch. To hurt.
> Madison's beautiful. A true delight.
> Wouldn't it be a shame if she came to harm?
> I could do that and so much more.
> But not yet.
> I shall bide my time.
> For you, you are the true prize.

Within the last six months, I'd received three of these letters; the other two both came in a similar fashion, hand-delivered to the office, addressed to me. No postmark. No return address. No hint as to who had sent them.

Nothing.

Like a ghost, the writer of these letters remained hidden.

It had to tie in with a case—the only explanation that made sense.

But they'd given no identifying clues. Nothing of note to clue me in on the author's true intentions or identity.

The content of the letters, though, had escalated. They asked whether I could feel their breath on my neck, something you had to be close to a person to experience.

In previous letters, they'd asked if I could feel their eyes watching me, something you could do from far away.

Whoever they were, they were growing bolder.

In my gut, I believed it came from somebody attached to The Syndicate. But the mention of Madison turned my stomach because if these letters were indeed from somebody involved with them, then they knew about her.

And she was in more danger than ever.

In a brief space of time, Madison had become all I cared about. The one I needed to keep safe and protect from all the bad people in the world, including her own mother.

How was I meant to do that if she wouldn't speak to me about what I witnessed?

But was I just as bad? Because my gut told me I wouldn't tell her about the letter, or about the fact the unknown writer had named her. Watched her.

I could handle whatever these pricks threw at me, but Madison, I worried about.

No matter what, I would keep Madison safe.

madison

SHOULD I REALISTICALLY BE SO SUPER EXCITED I could burst to be back at the office with Dylan?

No. No, I should not.

But there I sat, next to Dawn at her desk, more than thrilled to be back near him, even if for most of the morning I'd only spotted him from afar.

He had client meetings until three, so I passed my time helping Dawn with her admin tasks instead. If I had to be at the office, I may as well do something useful with my time.

Plus, Dawn had made fudge, as promised, so she was the current reigning champion in my good books.

At five minutes past three, Dawn turned to me on her swivel chair and smiled wide.

'Ah, would you look at this, Madison? I've got some paperwork here for Dylan to have a look over. Would you mind taking it to his office for me? My legs are all done in from my aqua aerobics last night.'

I smiled at her excuse. She'd already told me she spent

the previous evening lounging on her sofa watching reruns of Murder She Wrote.

'Sure,' I said, almost jumping off my chair. 'Don't want you hurting yourself further.'

She nodded in grave agreement.

With quick hellos to those I passed, I got to Dylan's office in record time.

Knock-knock.

No answer.

I knocked once more and still no answer. I'd paid enough attention to him to know his last clients for the day had left, so I wouldn't be walking in on an important meeting or anything like that.

The handle gave with little force, and the door unlocked.

An empty office greeted me.

I stepped inside and went over to his desk to place the paperwork on it, planning to put it down before taking up my usual spot in the armchair in the corner, but something in his pile of clutter caught my eye.

A typed letter, half poking out of a brown envelope.

Colour me intrigued.

Without a thought to the fact Dylan would come back at any point, I took the letter out and read it.

Then I re-read it straight away to make sure I hadn't imagined my name.

Nope. Clear as day.

Madison's beautiful. A true delight.

My heart raced. When did Dylan get it? And why hadn't he told me about it?

Surprise, shock, and hurt all rushed through me.

I poked inside the envelope and found another two

letters, typed in the same font and style. They didn't mention me, but they were threatening, nonetheless.

The door swung open, and I had no time to replace the letters where I found them.

'Hey, you,' Dylan said, coming through the door with two steaming mugs in his hands. 'Dawn said I'd find you in here. Hot chocolate?'

His eyes met mine, the smile leaching away from his face when he spotted the suspicion no doubt living in mine. He looked at the letter in my hand, then back to me.

'Everything okay?' he asked, entering the threshold and letting the door close shut firmly behind him. The noise reverberated through the room.

'What the fuck is this, Dill?' I asked, waving around the letter.

He shifted his weight but continued on his path to me, putting the mugs down on the small square of empty uncluttered space on his desk.

'Something you weren't meant to see.'

I rolled my eyes. He should teach a class: avoidance 101.

'Well, now I have seen them, so what are you going to do about it?'

He reached out to touch my arm, but I took a step back out of his grasp.

'I get you're mad because I didn't mention the threat against you, and for that, I'm sorry, but—'

'God, you're so dumb sometimes!' I threw my hands in the air in exasperation. 'I'm not mad because the letter mentions me.'

'Then why are you mad?' His eyebrows raised higher on his forehead, startled.

Bless him. He looked like an unsure creature, new to the world and so confused.

'I'm mad because you didn't tell me point blank! I'm mad because you've got it into your thick skull that I don't care about you. That I wouldn't want to know about something this important. That I wouldn't *care*! I want to know everything that's going on, Dylan, whether it has a direct impact on my life or not. If it bothers you, affects you, then I want to know about it. Because I do care about you. Too much, it would seem at times. I couldn't give a rat's arse that the letter mentions me!'

My breaths heaved out of me, my anger floating away the moment my speech ended, trailing off and leaving me embarrassed in its wake.

'I didn't want to worry you.'

'Well, instead of worrying me, you've pissed me off. Which do you think is worse?'

'Let's just—'

'Do not even *think* about finishing that sentence if it includes the phrase: let's move on and forget you saw it, or something to that effect.' I blinked, looking at him, maybe seeing him truly for the first time. No childish crush to filter my gaze. 'You protect me and make sure I'm safe, right?' He nodded. 'I want the same for you, Dill.'

'I know you do, but ...'

'But?'

'It's best I don't involve you more than necessary. For the both of us.'

My feelings boiled up and over. Every emotion aimed towards Dylan bubbled to the surface, yet instead of coming out in a kind way, it came out in an angry wave of words.

'I won't stand for it any longer, Dylan. I deserve to know things like this. You don't have the right to keep me in the dark.'

Dylan gripped his hair, the look he sent me like molten lava.

'Will you just shut up and kiss me.'

madison

WELL, NO NEED TO TELL ME TWICE.

Dylan's lips were on mine before I could take a full breath. He devoured me, completely and utterly, until my name left me, and I was putty in his hands.

His tongue, eager to join the party, sent shivers down my spine. Damn, Dylan Winters could kiss!

Even though his kisses were brutal and punishing, his large hand cupped my face gently, a juxtaposition I was more than happy to get behind.

'All I've thought of since seeing you again is kissing you,' he whispered, his breath on my face, the hushed tone of his voice enough to send me into overdrive.

Everything I'd ever wanted was happening right at that moment, and I could do nothing but blink back at him in awe.

Dylan chuckled, his heart thundering underneath my palm where it rested on his chest. His height meant I had to crane my neck a little to reach his lips, but no complaints would come from me.

An undeniable magnetism existed between us.

I'd always known about it, but Dylan had either ignored it or lived in denial. Stupid man.

'Stop talking about it and do more of it.'

He smiled, hearing the command within it. His lips recaptured mine, more demanding this time, and every nerve ending in my body came alive.

His hands roamed.

As did mine.

'We should probably wait until we get home,' he whispered, breaking the kiss again.

'Shhh.' I placed a finger against his lips. He bit it. 'Stop trying to stop.'

'But we're at the office.'

'So?' I reached up and nipped his bottom lip. 'The door's locked.'

Dylan's right eyebrow raised in question, and I swayed my hips as I walked to the door, making a show of locking it before coming back to stand before him.

'See.'

He chuckled, my nipples firming at the sound. His joy acted as my own personal aphrodisiac, and I wanted more of it.

'So it is,' he whispered against my lips, the nearness of him overwhelming. His hand travelled up my thigh, under my skirt, to tease the edges of my lace underwear. 'Wouldn't want somebody to come and spoil the fun.'

'I'm totally okay with coming,' I said back, breathless. It was bold, and a little scary, to tell him what I wanted. To put it out into the universe like that. I had experience, but not with anybody as mature or anybody I wanted as much as I wanted Dylan.

His wolfish smile in return made it worth it.

'I want you, Madison.' He kissed my neck. 'I want you to moan as I kiss you all over. I want you to open up for me like the good girl I know you are.'

Good girl? Why, when it came from his perfect mouth, did it sound so fucking hot?

He kissed my neck again, trailing kisses and soft caresses up and down.

'I've never done anything like this in my office before.' His eyes glinted with mischief. 'You're ruining me, Mads.'

'Or am I showing you what you've missed out on?' I bit my bottom lip, lowering my eyes until my eyelashes grazed my cheek.

Dylan paused. His finger tilted my chin up. 'The only thing I've missed out on is you.'

Damn.

His other finger, still poised at the edge of my underwear, teased the seam.

'Is this okay?' he asked, and I nodded.

Okay? Bloody hell, Dylan, it was what I wanted most in the world. Well, that and for him to realise we were meant to be together, but baby steps.

'Please,' I hushed out.

A squeak left my lips when his finger breached my entrance, my wetness from the build-up giving him no resistance.

One finger, two.

He whispered things in my ear I couldn't repeat, not

because I didn't remember them, but because I wanted to keep them all to myself. Save them for later.

I moaned, his finger curled against the bundle of nerves there, and my whole body shuddered.

Dylan's fingers were inside me, and we were at work, and oh my god, was this actually happening to me?

His fingers, with a skill I didn't want to question, worked expertly within me.

The orgasm built, climbing and climbing, until I couldn't hold back anymore.

His free hand covered my mouth in preparation for any noise I may make and fuck, that only made the whole thing hotter. More forbidden. As if it wasn't forbidden enough to mess around with somebody a lot older than you, not to mention your best friend's literal brother.

The thought of him being forbidden, mixed with the thought of me still being a teenager and him being thirty, sent me over the edge. I didn't want to analyse what that said about me, but my god, it was a major turn-on.

My release rocked through me, my moans stifled by his hand.

Dylan smiled at me. So beautiful, so handsome. 'Fuck, Mads. You're beautiful.'

The gradual comedown from my high, the way I felt better than ever. I never wanted the feeling to disappear. Nobody had ever made me feel so good, so wanted, so ... *alive.*

Dylan removed his hand from my underwear and brought it to his mouth, where he licked me off. *Oh my.*

Who knew he hid such a devilish demeanour?

'You taste like perfection.' He grinned wider. 'You *are* perfection.'

I took a step back, blinking at him, wondering if he'd put a stop to it all. Tell me we shouldn't be doing this and go cold on me.

But he didn't do that.

He stepped back, a dark smile on his face, his eyes glinting at me with a dare.

'Now I've come, it's only fair that you do too,' I said. 'I want to taste you.'

I reached out for him, and he shook his head. His hands were on the zip of his trousers. 'On your knees.'

dylan

MADISON WENT DOWN ONTO HER KNEES before me.

Only in my deepest fantasies had I imagined her on her knees in front of me, at work no less.

She took over, pushing my trousers and boxers down past my hips.

Her eyes lit up like they'd won a prize. How could I put it into words and actions that the winner was me?

My dick, now free of its constraints, was firmly within Madison's grasp. *Fuck.*

She poked her tongue out, licking the seam to taste the pre-cum beaded at the tip.

I hissed in a breath.

She repeated the action, a look of the devil in her eyes.

Then she licked me from the tip, all the way down my shaft and back again. Madison held all the power, and I merely lived within her orbit, hoping she'd never let me leave.

'Have I mentioned how fucking beautiful you are?' My words were coarse, hungry. I needed her to keep going. Her eyes caught mine; the eye contact was nearly enough for me to spill over too soon.

'You look pretty great from down here, too.' Madison watched me with smug delight. 'Maybe I should look at you from this angle more often.'

She truly was beautiful. But on her knees at my feet? Beautiful didn't even cover it. Everything about our actions was forbidden. Fuck, she wasn't even twenty, and yet I allowed this madness to continue.

Watching her come apart in my arms, to know my touch had that effect on her. Heaven.

My family would kill me if they found out.

Dottie would murder me, bury my body, and make sure nobody ever found me.

Was I ready to take this step? Fuck, I sort of didn't have much choice, with Madison's mouth wrapped around the head of my cock.

She took me in fully, and I let out a moan when I pressed the back of her throat.

Her dainty hand wrapped around the base, and with a firm grip, she moved her hand up and down, twisting it, bobbing her head as she did so.

'Just like that.' My hands went to the back of her head. Grounding me. 'Fuck, Madison. Your mouth feels so right wrapped around my cock.'

Nobody made me feel as alive as Madison Jones did.

Something about her spoke to me on a deeper level. No surface bullshit. When it comes to Madison, what you see is what you get.

Shit.

I had fallen into hell, and now there, I didn't want to claw my way out again.

The rightness of her mouth around me battled with the wrongness of it all.

I wanted her more than anything.

But I also wanted to keep things distant. *This* was the furthest thing from distance.

I should stop. Take my hands off the back of her head and apologise.

But I didn't do either of those things.

No.

I held her tighter, guiding her as she slid me deeper, her pace increasing.

Madison's eyes locked with mine, and the image of my cock disappearing into her mouth, her eyes on me, nearly had me losing my control.

From the little breaths and moans leaving my lips, she could tell I would come soon.

And she matched me with fervour.

The head of my cock hit the back of her throat again, and she gagged a little.

'Make me come,' I whispered, our eyes still locked together. 'Swallow my cum and taste me the way I've tasted you.'

Her blue eyes widened. She smiled around me, picking up the speed of her twisting hand, until the first ribbons of cum shot into her mouth.

'Fuck, fuck, fuck.'

She swallowed every last drop.

'You're such a good girl.'

Madison got up from her knees and trailed her mouth up my body, to my neck, to my mouth, kissing as she went.

I kissed the taste of me from her lips.

How on earth could I keep my distance from her now?

madison

THE MORNING AFTER THE NIGHT BEFORE.

I'd always hoped once Dylan saw me, things would slot into place on their own. Natural. Without force.

But waking up in my bed alone told me a different story. One of regret, avoidance.

Something Dylan Winters was extremely adept at.

When I'd stirred a few hours before, we were wrapped up in one another, my leg draped over his hips. Slotted together the way I'd dreamed of so many times. And even though we'd woken this way a bit recently, after the escapades of the previous evening, it hit differently.

After we got home from the office, nothing more happened. Things had cooled down by then, but there wasn't anything awkward about it.

We'd turned a corner, or so I thought.

Once again, Dylan proved me wrong.

I got out of bed and made my way to the kitchen, only fifty per cent ready to face him and start my day. Maybe his getting up before me wasn't a snub. Maybe he'd decided to start on breakfast and treat me. Or he planned to wake me up with a kiss and a hot chocolate and I had woken before he could.

Maybe ...

The atmosphere in the kitchen stopped my wondering.

Dylan, although moving around the kitchen and making breakfast, gave off shifty vibes.

'Morning,' I said, hoping it'd shatter the atmosphere.

It did not.

'Morning,' he mumbled, grabbing a pan out of the cupboard and placing it on the hob. 'Want scrambled eggs on toast?'

'Please.' I filled up an empty glass from the draining board with water from the fridge. 'Need me to help with anything?'

'No, I've got it, thanks.'

'Okay ...'

'Take a seat, and I'll bring your food over when it's done.'

I went and took a seat on the sofa, not wanting to hover when he'd made it clear he didn't want me near him.

Maybe pretending nothing happened between us was for the best.

Dylan clearly regretted it, and I wasn't going to once again put myself out there when I'd done it multiple times already.

Who knew somebody as good-looking and genuinely nice as Dylan could make me feel so crappy about myself?

I hated myself for how much I was letting it get to me.

It was at times of despair that I wished I acted more like

Dottie. That girl never let anything bother her, and if she did, you'd never know it. Gosh, even as her best friend, I'd only seen her truly upset three times. The first was when somebody from school fell off a climbing frame and cracked their head open—not a pleasant sight—but mainly, she was more upset about the fact she'd seen it versus the person being hurt. The second time was when Nathan ended things—a rather dark day in Dottie World. And lastly, the day my dad died, she cried because I was one step closer to being free of all their bullshit.

Dottie Winters cared about me, even if she showed it in ways others couldn't understand or found odd, and she'd be so pissed off if she found out we shared a bed, let alone that I gave him head.

Maya Angelou once said, 'When someone shows you who they are, believe them the first time.'

I'd let Dylan show me more than once.

And I made a vow to be more cautious in the future.

THE NEXT DAY CAME, and Dylan and I were still in an awkward stage of barely talking, yet still spending all our time together. *Make it make sense.*

After he'd made me breakfast, we'd watched TV on the sofa, making the odd comment about something or other, and we spent the day in an uncomfortable cloud.

Then, when bedtime came, we got into bed and fell asleep as two separate beings—who still found themselves wrapped together like vines come morning.

'I'm off to visit Dahlia today,' he said, coming out of the

bathroom dressed for the day in casual grey joggers and a white T-shirt.

Drool threatened to leave my mouth, and I wiped the corner of it just in case.

'Okay.'

'So I've asked Dana and Dottie to stop by.'

'You have?' I sat up straighter on the sofa, angling my body so I could look at him better. 'I don't need babysitters, Dylan.'

'I know,' he said, attempting to placate me. 'But I hate the thought of you being here alone, especially after that man hung around outside. We still have no clue who he is or whether he's linked to The Syndicate.'

I opened my mouth to explain that whole situation away, but in order to do that, I'd have to tell him about my mum showing up—something I hadn't told him about on purpose. Best to keep quiet. Yes, that contradicted my stance on lies, but needs must.

'Well, thanks,' I murmured, turning my attention back to the TV in the hopes that he'd leave sooner.

The door closed softly behind him, and I let out a deep breath.

But of course, I had barely any time to sit and think about everything because Dottie and Dana arrived within ten minutes of Dylan's departure.

'Hello,' Dana called, stepping through the door and wiping her shoes on the mat before taking them off. 'Dylan called and said you needed watching.'

I sputtered a laugh. 'Yep, something like that. Glad you two were available at such short notice.'

'I know you love spending time with our parents, but we

thought it'd be best for you to hang around with people your own age who aren't about to drop down dead. And yes, I'm including Dylan in that.' Dottie flounced inside, throwing her jacket over the back of the sofa before throwing herself onto said sofa. 'Well, this is new!'

… Ah! The sofa.

'Do you like it?' I couldn't contain my glee.

'Love!' Dana hung Dottie's jacket up on the hooks. 'When did you get it?'

'Dylan and I went and picked it out last weekend. My old one had seen better days.'

Dana nodded, her face twisted in thought. 'It's beautiful, sure, but it doesn't look comfortable for our dear brother. Surprised his *bad back* hasn't given up on him completely if he's staying on this thing.'

My head snapped in her direction to be met with a vindictive smile.

Dottie was oblivious as usual to the implication. 'Dylan's a big boy. I'm sure he can handle it.'

'I'm sure he can,' Dana said. 'But I'm not sure he has to, right, Mads?'

If looks could kill, then Dana Winters would have died on the spot.

I bit my tongue, not wanting to say anything to alert Dot to what was really being said between us. Dottie's phone, lit up to show her social feed, had her attention more than me or Dana did.

Maybe Dana noticed the fire burning in my gaze, or maybe she decided to choose life instead of a pyre. Either way, she took up her spot beside Dottie and said, 'Have I mentioned I hate Isaac Wilson with a passion?'

dylan

Acting a coward didn't suit me, yet I did it anyway.

And from the look Dahlia gave me when she opened the door, it became clear she thought so too.

'Why is your sorry arse standing in my doorway on a Sunday afternoon?'

'Technically, it's still my doorway as we own this place together, remember?'

She waved me off and opened the door wider for me to step inside. 'Semantics.'

'Can't I be here because I miss you?' I said, the smell of the place once so familiar to me all of a sudden, like a stranger. I scrunched my nose and sniffed. 'Dottie's been using her incense.' It came out as an accusation.

'You've not been here to tell her no,' Dahlia snapped, then smiled sheepishly. 'Sorry. It's just when we agreed to live with her, we were both gonna be here to rein her in, you know? But without you here, it's a lot harder to keep her in check.'

'She's a handful,' I agreed. 'But the only way we'll get a handle on her antics is if we put our foot down.'

'I know, I know.' Dahlia walked into the kitchen, and I followed. 'Want a drink?'

'I'd love an Americano,' I said. 'Madison doesn't have a barista-style machine, so I've been making do with instant coffee. Believe me, it is not the same.'

'I bet.' She went about making the drink, then handed me a steaming mug. The smell hit my nose, and my mouth watered.

'Oh, how I've missed you,' I whispered. Dahlia raised an eyebrow but remained silent. 'Don't judge me. My life's changed in a flash.'

'And there was me thinking it had changed for the better.'

The two of us migrated to the breakfast bar.

'What's that supposed to mean?'

'You tell me,' she nudged. She wanted me to say something, to admit to something, but surely, she wasn't referring to my *thing* with Madison. If you could even call it that.

I feigned ignorance. When in doubt, act oblivious. 'What's there to tell?'

'Oh, come off it, Dylan. I'm your sister, and I know you better than anyone. We've lived together for six years, for starters.'

'Maybe if you ask me specific questions, I'll be able to give specific answers.'

'Hmm ...' Dahlia took a sip of her coffee, her eyes staring out the window that overlooked our garden. Or maybe she was focused on the raindrops as they slid down the glass, growing larger as they joined their friends on the way. 'How do you feel about Madison?'

Oh, great. She'd started off with a heavy hitter.

'That's extremely broad.'

'And you're extremely vague.'

I rolled my eyes. 'I care about her,' I admitted. 'But you know that already.'

'And?'

'And I don't want her to get hurt, of course.'

'Of course.'

'Will you stop that?'

Dahlia blew out a breath between her gritted teeth. 'You like her, don't you?'

'Well, of course I like her. I've always liked her.'

Dahlia rolled her eyes, hard. 'No, dipshit. I mean, you *like* her, in more than an oh-she's-like-my-sister kind of a way.'

The sentence settled over me. Rooted down deep.

Shit.

Dahlia spoke true.

I opened my mouth to protest, unsure exactly what I could say to defend myself, but she cut me off before I could.

'Just listen, dickhead. No interjections until I've finished, all right?'

I nodded, thoroughly chastised. Dahlia may be two years younger than me, but there were plenty of times when she acted like the long-suffering elder sibling.

'It's quite clear you like the girl, and don't give me any bullshit by denying it. Ever since life threw you two together, I've seen a new sparkle in your eye. Before Madison, you worked, you worked out, and you came home to crash before doing it all again. For fuck's sake, Dill, you actually came to a bowling tournament for once because it meant spending more time with her.'

'I—'

'I said no interjections!' Dahlia turned her narrowed gaze to me and didn't look away. 'I know you're not sleeping on the sofa.'

'H-how?' I sputtered, but she only intensified her evil glare.

'A sister knows all, and I've seen the way the two of you look at each other. Act around each other. And I'm sure you're telling yourself it's only because you care about her like you always have. That the only reason you're spending so much time with her is because it's the right thing to do and because your job has demanded it of you.'

She took a deep breath, losing a little of the steam she'd had at the start.

'But that's utter bull, and you know it. The only reasons I'd even consider valid as to why you're not making things work with her are because of her age or because of Dottie. She turns twenty next month. Get over yourself. You're not ancient, Dylan. You're thirty.'

'And what about Dottie?'

'Well, she can get over herself, too!' Dahlia slammed her hand down on the black marble counter. 'Look, if you and Madison give this thing a go and it doesn't work out, at least you tried and you can both move on. But this limbo the two of you are stuck in? It'll never go away. It's not something you can sweep under the rug and avoid for eternity.'

Her words lingered in the air after she said them, waiting

for me to pick them up, take them in, and listen to them. Truly listen.

'I've messed up.'

'Duh.'

I knocked her shoulder. 'Something ... happened the other night, and instead of talking to her about it, I ignored her, pretended it never took place.'

'You are dim, aren't you?'

'Well aware, thanks.' I sighed. 'When I go home, I'll apologise. Talk to her properly. Find out if she wants the same as me.' Even though I didn't know exactly what I wanted.

Dahlia laughed at that. 'Dill, she's always wanted it.'

'Right ...' I looked to the window, to the raindrops, no longer falling but stationary.

The idea of talking to Madison, putting everything out into the open, scared me.

When Caroline ended things the way she did, and my only reaction was one of sheer relief, it made me question myself as a partner.

Could I put Madison before work, before ambition, before ... everything?

I wanted to.

I was ready to.

And the moment I got home, I would tell her.

CHAPTER 35

dylan

MAYBE I STAYED AWAY A LITTLE LONGER THAN intended.

Every time Dahlia gave me a nudge to leave, I found a reason to stay longer.

Oh, I need to grab something from my room.

I should probably check on the meters while I'm here.

Do you think we need to talk about changing the tiles in the downstairs bathroom?

By the time I got in my car, I had Dahlia threatening to murder me in quite creative and unapologetic ways. Pretty sure she meant them, too.

I found Madison at home curled up on our new sofa, tucked under a fleece blanket, watching a comfort film of hers on the TV. She mouthed along, knowing every line, and I stopped to smile at my view. The fact I'd never referred to the new green sofa as *hers* instead of *ours* told me all I needed to work up the courage to talk to her.

I could get used to coming home to her. For real, and not because of a case or some kind of forced circumstance.

'Hey,' she said, her voice muffled by the blanket. 'Dottie and Dana didn't leave too long ago, so don't worry, my babysitters did no wrong. You can transfer their payment.'

I made my way over to the sofa, and Madison shifted her legs so they curled closer to her, leaving room for me to take a seat on the empty cushion.

'I'm sorry for making you feel like a kid that can't be trusted to stay home alone.'

She waved my apology off. 'Honestly, Dill, I'm not even mad about it. I was in a bad mood this morning, that's all.'

'No, I'm being serious,' I said, taking her soft hand in mine. 'I acted, no, have been acting, like a total dick, and you don't deserve any of it.' Her hand twitched in mine, and I squeezed it softly. 'I'm the one acting like a child. You told me we should talk and be adults about all this'—I waved my free hand, gesturing around the room—'but instead, I've avoided you and pretended nothing happened. That noth-ing's *happening*.' The emphasis felt important. 'But some-thing *is* happening, and I've been too scared to face it.'

'I'm not sure I understand ...'

'I think ... I think we'll be good together. If you want to try, that is?'

Madison's head snapped up to look at me, her mouth agape.

'Seriously, Dylan, you're so dumb sometimes. I've been trying to show you that for the last month!'

'I know, I know.'

'I'm worried you'll change your mind again.' She shook her head. 'Every time we kiss, I expect things to change, and they haven't.'

'I've come to my senses, Mads.' I grabbed her ankles and

placed her legs over my lap, slowly massaging her calf. 'I vow to stop acting a fool.'

'Is that something a person can vow?'

'I'm doing it anyway.' We both laughed, and the sound of her chuckle settled in my stomach. A good feeling. 'Do you forgive me for acting a fool?'

Madison took a deep breath. 'I do. I understand you can't help being a fool sometimes. It's the way you're made.'

'So this is happening ...' I trailed off.

The smile she gave me knocked me back. '*We* are happening.'

THAT FIRST DAY, things were a little unsure, like neither of us knew how to all of a sudden be dating. But when night came, and we could snuggle up next to one another rather than keeping our distance, things fell into place rather quickly.

'Morning,' Madison said, coming into the kitchen dressed for the day.

She reached up to kiss my cheek as if she'd done so every morning, and the casualness of it all struck me. Every morning could be like this.

'Morning.' Steam rose from the two mugs on the counter, and I smiled when she picked up her hot chocolate. 'Sleep well?'

'The best sleep I've had in ages,' she said with a small smile. 'Was nice to not worry, ya know? For the last week, I've not wanted to turn around in fear you were facing me and it'd get awkward fast.'

'Don't. I've basically been a log staring up at the ceiling.'

We both laughed at how silly our actions were when looked back upon them.

'Least it's all sorted now,' Madison said, rinsing out her now empty mug. That girl drank hot chocolate before it even cooled. 'We off to the office?'

'We are. I need to grab some bits from Dahlia's on the way back later.'

Neither of us acknowledged the fact I no longer referred to that place as home.

Things were easier that way.

Remind me to tell you about what your mum said when I get home.

Can't you message it now? I'm intrigued.

Nope. Way too long to type, and it'll make more sense in person, I promise. Only two hours to go until I see your face.

Two hours too long.

Oh, hush up. Get back to work so you can get home to me.

Your wish is my command.

I PLACED a kiss on the top of Madison's head, breathing in the scent of her vanilla shampoo, a scent I now smelt like, too.

'What are we going to watch now?' I asked.

The two of us had finished the series we were making our way through each night, and it had left a gap in our routine.

'I was thinking we could watch that baking competition,' she replied. 'There's a celebrity series out now.'

'Any celebrities we actually know?' I doubted it. Pop culture wasn't my strong suit.

'Think Bridger Daniels is in it, and that other guy from that show I love.'

'Nice and vague, Mads.'

She laughed, the sound musical. 'Oh, you know the one I mean! You'll recognise him the moment the episode starts.'

'Okay.' I placed another kiss on her head. 'Baking it is.'

'HOW MUCH GARLIC did you put in that pan?'

Madison and I were cooking together, hard to do in such a small space, but we were making it work.

Kind of nice to cook with her. Intimate.

'Only a little,' she replied, mixing it in with the onion.

'The recipe calls for two cloves. Pretty sure you used an entire bulb.'

'What can I say? I've a weakness for garlic.'

The laugh burst from me, taking us both by surprise. 'A weakness for garlic.'

'Yes.' She paused and placed the hand with the spatula on her hip. 'Is there a problem with that?'

'No. No problem.' My hands were out flat in front of me. 'I'm only saying that later, when the kisses aren't coming, you'll know what's to blame.'

She nodded her head in solemnity. 'My weakness for garlic.'

'Right!'

A WEEK PASSED in the blink of an eye.

And during that week, something lightened in me.

A light, not present before, appeared and gripped me with all its power.

All because of Madison.

And sure, a week wasn't a long enough time to decide on a future, wasn't a long enough time to make any deep decisions.

But one thing became apparent to me, something I couldn't deny.

I was falling for Madison in a way I'd never fallen for anyone before.

And the wrath of Dottie became something quite insignificant under the blinding light of Madison's smile.

madison

DYLAN'S BREATHING UNDER MY EAR CALMED ME. Settled me the way no other thing did.

He'd fallen asleep while we watched some baking programme, and even though his breathing threatened to take me under, too, I needed to keep watching to learn if my favourite actor won best baker.

A week had passed since Dylan asked me if I wanted to see where things went between us, and my, what a week it had been.

Things had fallen into place in a way that still felt a little unreal to me. Like I'd stumbled into a favourite romance film and found myself the heroine getting everything she'd ever wanted.

At no point had I tired of spending time with him. Being around him. Getting to know him better.

Sure, I'd known him for years, but he had always existed through the lens of a childish crush, rather than as a real, actual human.

Lucky for me, I liked the real, actual human better.

'So I've been working on this case for the last two years.'

'Long time, then.'

He nodded, coming around his desk to pull me into his arms and against his muscular body. 'Before you ... saw what you did ... I thought we were going to have to throw the towel in.'

'Well, yay for you rejecting me.'

He laughed, the vibrations travelling through to me. 'Is that what happened?'

'Er, yes!' I poked his pec. 'I asked you out on a date and you said no. Safe to call that a rejection, methinks.'

'Hmm ...' His hands trailed from where they rested on my hips to squeeze my bum. 'Looks like it's all worked out for the best, wouldn't you say?'

I pushed my weight onto my tiptoes and reached up to kiss his lips.

Kisses, or at least Dylan's kisses, were worth dying for.

Dramatic? Yes, but oh so very true.

For years, I'd dreamed of kissing his lips, and now I got to on a daily basis, I wouldn't do anything to stop it, like telling Dottie.

The man could kiss.

He could also do something rather nice with his fingers, too ...

'Bowling this Sunday.'

'Right.' Dylan came and sat beside me on the sofa, putting his arm out so I could snuggle up against him. 'How are we gonna act?'

'How should I know?' I laughed. 'Pretty sure they're all aware of my giant crush on you. You've always acted oblivious, so maybe it's you who needs to act, not me.'

'Oblivious?'

'Yes! You never gave any indication you knew about it.'

'I didn't want to embarrass you.' He ran his hand through his hair. 'Also, I didn't think of you in that way and thought it'd be best to ignore and avoid.'

I laughed. 'Yeah, that's fair. Should thank you for that actually. If I'd known you were aware, I'd have died on the spot. Your dad would've had to mop my remains up from between lanes seven and eight.'

'Well, isn't it a good thing that never happened?'

'It proper is.' I kissed his chest. 'How else would I get to beat you in this upcoming game?'

He tickled my side, setting me off into giggles. 'You're going down, Jones.'

'WHAT HAPPENS to me if Malcolm Silver pleads not guilty and this all has to go to trial?'

'A long wait is what.' Dylan's grumble had me smiling. It always made me smile to realise how little of the real Dylan he showed to other people and how much he permitted me to witness now. 'Not like we've waited enough as it is.'

'Will I have to appear in court?'

He nodded. 'Yeah, but if you don't want to be in the

room or seen, then you could do it via a stream to hide your identity.'

'Pretty sure they know of my identity already.' The threatening letter with my name inside still sat on Dylan's desk. He'd told me he hadn't mentioned the letters to his bosses, but Noah knew. He'd received some, too.

'Maybe. I'd still rather you not become top of their hit list.'

'Dill, it'll be fine. The police will protect me if anything happens, and so will you.'

'I don't want you to get hurt.'

'I won't,' I promised.

Neither of us voiced how stupid a promise it was.

dylan

It started with Dahlia.

A look, a smile, that said: *you're not so good at secrets, Dylan Winters.*

Of course it started with Dahlia. She, unlike the others the look moved on to, knew the truth. She'd told me to go after Madison, finally get my shit together, and pursue a relationship.

Clearly, something in our actions towards each other, or maybe the way Madison's hand grazed my arm when returning from a bowl, let Dahlia in on the secret for definite.

Before the evening, she'd assumed, but now, she believed it was confirmed.

Touching Madison in front of my family was a bad idea, but whenever she entered my bubble, I found myself unable to stop.

My body wanted to be near hers. It was a gravitational pull too strong to fight.

But more than that, I wanted to be near her in any

capacity. To listen to her laugh. To watch her eyes wrinkle at the edges when she found some anecdote or other particularly amusing.

'So things have sorted themselves out between the two of you, ay?' Dahlia whispered when the two of us were out of earshot of everybody else.

'Is it obvious?' I snuck a glance back towards where Madison and Dottie were laughing about a shared acquaintance.

Dahlia laughed. 'I mean, I'm in the know, so maybe I'm seeing things because of that. But ...'

'But?'

'Mum's got her eyes on you two, so beware. You know what she's like. She'll have you married off in her head before the evening's over.'

'Good thing neither Madison nor I want to get married then, isn't it?'

Dahlia's jaw dropped. 'Have I missed something?'

I stared back blankly.

'You two must have spoken deeply enough for you to state that with such certainty.' She smiled, her purple lipstick complementing her well. Not that I'd compliment her now after tormenting me. 'I'm surprised. Happy.'

'Do you think Dottie's spotted anything amiss?'

'Dottie would have to be thinking about somebody other than herself.' Dahlia clapped me on the shoulder. 'I think you're safe, bro.'

I chuckled. Dahlia looked over my shoulder, and her smile grew wider, a feat I hadn't thought possible, but clearly, what did I know?

'I'm gonna take these drinks over to the lanes.' Dahlia lifted the tray and nodded before heading off.

Without turning around, I knew who I'd see.

Bonnie Winters.

A formidable woman for somebody so short, stood there looking at me with the biggest smile.

'Is there anything you want to share, darling?' she asked, the glint in her eyes telling me plenty.

Two options were available to me: deny or defend.

Or maybe an answer in between.

'What about?' I asked.

'Oh, don't give me that tosh, Dylan. I'm your mother. I can see right through you!'

It always amazed me how one sentence from her could make me feel seven years old all over again. Chastised and unable to take action without it being known by her first.

'Okay, okay.' I put my hands up in defence. 'We may or may not be dating.'

Mum squealed and grabbed my hands in hers, gripping them tight. 'I've waited a long time for you to tell me.'

'A long time ... Mum, it only happened like two weeks ago!'

She hummed. 'If you say so.'

I laughed because if I didn't, I'd fold and give in and talk to my mum about things I hadn't told anyone. Like how much I was falling for Madison.

'How did you know to ask tonight anyway?' My eyes narrowed.

'A mother knows these things, dear.' Mum rubbed my cheek, all soothing-like. 'Of course I'd hoped you two would happen, and I was certain one day it *would* happen, but I couldn't be sure of the exact timing.'

'What made you so positive it'd happen?'

'Madison's been crushing on you for a very long time, dear.' Mum smiled, memories fogging her gaze. 'I knew one day you'd notice her for who she truly is. Beautiful, inside and out.'

Beautiful, inside and out.

Mum had wrapped Madison up in a bow with only four words.

'She is, isn't she?' I murmured, looking back at Madison, still acting goofy with Dottie. The two of them had such a unique friendship, at times I often wondered if my relationship with her would ever measure up. 'Do you think Dot will kill us?'

'I think you've got some time yet until you need to tell Dottie.' Mum laughed. 'You could probably tell her in a year's time and it would somehow still blindside her.'

***

'BIT OF A SORE LOSER, aren't you?' I ruffled Madison's hair, and she darted her hand out to stop me.

'I am not a sore loser! I prefer winning, that's all.'

The car lit up when I unlocked the doors.

Bowling with the family was always fun, and now I was no longer holding myself back from liking Madison, it was even better.

By the end of the evening, the whole family was giving me *the look*.

Everybody except Dottie, of course.

'Did you feel Dana staring at us?' Mads asked once we were both safe and snug inside the car, away from my family's earwigging. 'If looks could burn, she'd have left a black hole in the back of my skull. Pretty sure she suspects.'

'Well, Dahlia outright asked me so ...'

'She did?' Madison put a strand of her blonde hair behind her ear, her face deep in thought.

'Yep. Oh, and Mum knows, too.'

'Of course she does.' Mads shook her head. 'Your mum has seen through me since the day she met me.'

'Isn't it so spine-tingling when she knows you better than you even know yourself?'

'Right!' Mads smacked her hand on her knee. 'Every time, I wonder if she talks to spirits to get her information. It's the only explanation I've come to that makes sense.'

We fell silent as I turned the key, the engine rumbling to life, and we pulled out of the parking space.

Everything in my life had fallen into place over the last few weeks. Work, Madison, my family. All of it.

It hit me how much I'd missed out on by holing myself up in the office, avoiding life and the joy you can have, all because I cared more about work than anything else.

'I had a good time tonight, Dill.' Mads's hand found mine and wrapped around it. 'Even if I lost to you.'

'I'm glad you being around meant I got back into all this. I let work and Caroline stop me from being with my family, and I hate myself for it.'

'Don't be too hard on yourself. We've all done things we're not proud of to avoid reality.'

I wondered if she was referring to her mum showing up

—an event she still hadn't confided in me about. I should approach it and get her to open up.

Maybe too fragile a topic for a Sunday night, though, and I supposed it could wait until a later date.

All I had to do was stand by her, support her, and then maybe she'd open up without my having to pry.

I wanted there to be no secrets left between us.

And I could wait a little longer for that day to come.

madison

Knock-knock.

A look through the peephole told me exactly who stood on the other side of my front door, and believe me, I didn't want to open it.

Almost didn't open it.

But if I didn't, she'd probably kick up a fuss and start hollering and shouting and causing a nuisance of herself.

It wasn't fair to interrupt other people's lives because my mother hadn't a nice bone in her body.

Or worse, Doris would tell Dylan, thinking she was protecting me, and I didn't want him finding out from somebody else. The fact Mum had shown up a second time told me I needed to share things with Dylan and explain this mess.

'Madison! Oi, you little brat, open up!' Mum's voice came through the wood, the sound of her voice enough to have me close to crumbling to the floor, to cover my ears to block her out. Block everything out.

But I wasn't ten anymore and too scared to stand up for myself.

I flung the door open. 'What do you want?' I snarled.

'Is that any way to greet your own mother?' Her top lip curled in disgust.

'You stopped having the right to call yourself that the moment you hit me the first time.'

'Do I look like the kind of woman to hit her own child?'

'Do you really want me to answer that?' My eyes assessed her, travelling from head to toe, and a chill shivered down my spine. Only three weeks had passed since she last darkened my doorstep, yet she looked even worse now.

'What are you doing here?' I put both my hands on the door, holding it firm.

'Ralph told me he'd get your attention, but as usual, I have to do everything for myself around here.'

Ralph? Lord only knew who that was. Some shady character she'd befriended in the darkest of alleys, no doubt. She never attracted savoury types.

Her hair, stringy as ever, was missing from certain parts of her scalp, large bald patches visible instead. Her front tooth—her last remaining tooth on the top—was also missing.

Shame I couldn't bring myself to pity her.

'Madison, darling.' Her gummy smile didn't inspire warmth. 'Mummy needs some help.'

I almost admired her change of tact.

Almost.

'What do you want?' I repeated my earlier question. If I let her get into my head, she'd derail the conversation right off the track, and I couldn't have that.

'Money,' she blurted.

'Money,' I said. 'How much money?'

'I—' Her pupils darted around, not focusing on any one spot. 'You see … I've got myself into a spot of bother.'

'A spot of bother.' My tone was dull.

'Are you gonna repeat everything I say, you stupid bitch?' she snapped. Ah, so there she was. She'd never been able to hide her true self for long. It always came out, even when she tried oh so very hard to keep it buried down deep.

I deserved better than this.

I started to close the door, but Mum put all her strength into keeping it open.

'Please, Madison.' She blinked at me. 'Before you shut me out.'

'You've got precisely five minutes before I shut the door in your face, regardless of whether your fingers are in the way. Got it?'

She nodded her agreement.

I opened it a fraction. 'Who do you owe money to?'

'Bad people.'

An eye roll threatened, but I held it back. Funny enough, I didn't think it was the only eye-roll-worthy thing she'd say, so it seemed best to hold it back for something worthwhile. Save them up, as it were.

'What kind of bad people?'

'The kind who'd kill you and throw your body into the river.'

'Lakeland doesn't have a river.'

'The lake then,' she said, her frustration with me climbing.

'And how much do you owe them?'

'Ten grand.'

'Ten grand?' My tone was incredulous. 'How the fuck do you owe ten grand? Who would be stupid enough to give you that much money?'

'Technically they didn't.'

'Of course they didn't,' I muttered, the information running through my head at a speed hard to keep up with. 'What you're actually here to tell me is that you *stole* ten grand from some very bad people.'

She stayed silent.

'Whatever you did, however much you owe, it isn't my problem. I'm not gonna bail you out of this one, Mum. You've got to figure it out for yourself.'

'You ungrateful wretch! Your daddy was right about you. We should've got rid of you when we had the chance.'

'Get away from my home or I'll call the police.'

No more would I listen to her filth. She didn't deserve me, never had, and I wasn't about to let myself wallow because she'd never acted the way a mum should.

The fact she thought I'd even have ten grand to spare for her made me laugh.

Sure, I'd done well with my social media, but I'd tied a lot of it up in savings and investments. Luckily, I had savings, seeing as I couldn't currently work because of everything going on.

'You wouldn't.'

'Try. Me.'

For the second time, I slammed the door in her face.

By the time Dylan arrived home, the fight had left me.

My whole body was numb, and I didn't want to face him, but I knew I had to. I couldn't avoid the situation any longer. I hated lies and myself when I told them.

'Hey,' he said. 'Everything okay today?'

I'd convinced him I'd be fine spending the day at home without him for one day. As much as I loved spending time with him, it was good to have our own space, too. No sketchy people had shown up in the last three weeks and everything had returned to normal, at least on the surface. No more letters had arrived at his office either.

After an hour of talking it over, he'd agreed.

Once I told him about Mum's visit, though, he'd change his mind and never agree again.

And I was going to tell him. I was ready to open up— face the world and my place in it.

Dylan came and sat beside me on the sofa, opening his arm so I could snuggle into his side.

'I've got something I need to tell you,' I whispered.

madison

I INHALED, EXHALED.

'My mum showed up today.'

Dylan's body went still beside me, but he remained quiet, waiting for me to continue.

'It's actually the second time she's shown up this month.'

He made a hmm-ing noise but still said nothing.

'I know I should've told you earlier, but fuck, Dill, I was so, so embarrassed. Your parents are the literal best things on this earth and my remaining one is the scum living under the surface.'

Dylan shuffled his body so he could look at my face. The shame written there for all to see.

'I'm sorry,' I mumbled.

'You don't have to be sorry,' he said, wiping away a tear from my cheek. *Oh, when did they start?*

'But I do.' My bottom lip wobbled. 'I didn't tell you, and you've been so nice to me.'

'I already knew about your mum coming to visit, Mads.'

My heart dropped out of the bottom of my body. Flopped around on the floor at my feet. Metaphorically. Seeing as I was sitting down on the sofa with my feet curled up underneath me.

'You did?' My voice was barely audible. Embarrassed.

'Yeah. I've been waiting for you to tell me, but I'm not mad. I get why you don't want to talk about her.'

'She owes some bad people ten grand. Wanted me to give it to her. Also, she implied she'd sent a man called Ralph around to talk to me. I guess he's the bald man I rang you all scared about.' I let out a bitter laugh. 'There I was thinking the worst, but nope, just a lackey of my mum's.'

He whistled. 'Ten grand? Jeez.'

'I know,' I moaned. 'Who does she even know with that kind of money?'

'People do a lot of stupid things when they're desperate.'

'Yeah, I suppose.' The words tumbled out, real and raw. 'My whole life, I wished I had different parents. Or that the hospital made a mistake giving me to them, and my real family would swoop in one day and save me.' I laughed at the naivety of childhood me. 'Fully believed my Miss Honey would arrive, and I'd escape ... everything.'

Even at nearly twenty, the same wistfulness filled me whenever I thought of there being a whole other life and family out there for me. Silly, yet there, nonetheless.

Dylan's hand rubbed my shoulder in a circular motion. 'I'm gonna sort it, Mads. I promise.'

'How?'

'I'll talk to her.' His thumb moved to rub my lower lip. 'You can trust me with this.'

I blinked, lost in his dark brown eyes. 'Do you think it'll actually make a difference?'

'I'm a lawyer, babe. She'll listen to me.'

The rest of his sentence swarmed into a low buzzing because the way he'd ever so casually called me babe had stolen my focus, flashing in my mind like a beacon. *Swoon.*

On impulse, I kissed his cheek.

'What was that for?' His smile lit me up inside.

'Just 'cause.' I bit my bottom lip, my attempt at acting coy. 'I think you're rather handsome.'

'You do?' Dylan chuckled. 'That's a good thing, to be honest, because I think you're beautiful.'

My lips found his once more, and this time, it wasn't a mere peck of the lips. No, it was a full-on attack.

He met me with equal vigour. Our conversation died off, the wants of our bodies more important than discussing anything else.

We broke apart, and I whispered, 'Let's take this to our room.'

Our room. A phrase new to us, but one that felt so right.

He looked at me, concern lingering in his eyes, fighting the want also swimming there. 'Are you sure? You've had quite the day.'

'I've never been more sure of anything.'

dylan

MADISON LAY ON THE BED, LOOKING BACK AT ME, and I needed a moment to collect myself.

The moment we entered our bedroom, I froze.

'Are you okay?' she asked, concern thick in her eyes.

'I'm okay,' I replied, my voice barely above a whisper. 'I just ...'

'You just what?'

I laughed. Or was it more of a choke?

'I don't know.' I chuckled again. 'It's all I've thought about for weeks.'

'So why are you standing there, still as a statue?' A smile played on her lips, but her eyes were assessing me. Wary. 'If you don't want to, we can—'

'No,' I cut her off. 'I want to. Fuck, Mads, I *really* want to.'

She moved up the bed, placing her back up against the headboard. 'Talk to me, then. Tell me what's up.'

'Nothing's up,' I said, trying to sound calmer than my

racing thoughts. 'I don't want to mess this up. This means a lot to me.'

Her eyes softened.

'It means a lot to me, too.' She bit her bottom lip, not in a seductive way, but in a self-conscious way. 'I like you, Dylan. Like, *really* like you. Pretty sure my actions have made that super obvious, but in case you were confused or unsure ... I hope that clears it up.'

'I like you, too. More than I've ever liked anybody, honestly.' The words tumbled out of me without permission, but once they were out there, I didn't want to take them back. Madison deserved to know the truth, especially with what we were about to do.

'I'm glad.'

Mads got up from the bed and walked over to where I'd paused in the doorway. Her eyes glowed with something I couldn't decipher.

With a slowness I admired, she lifted her dress over her hips, revealing each inch of skin to me like a prize only I had a right to. Underneath, she wore a matching set of black lace underwear, and the way it contrasted with her pale skin set my heart on fire.

'You're beautiful,' I said in awe. 'Have I ever told you that?'

'You may have mentioned it once or twice,' she said, an irresistibly devastating grin arresting my attention. 'But I'm always game for you to say it again.'

'Oh, yeah?'

She tilted her head, an admission. 'Before you, I always thought of myself as the plain one. Passable, pleasant, but bland.' Her arms, covered in goosebumps, pulled me closer. 'But you, you make me look at myself in a new light.'

I kissed her, injecting it with all that burned inside me in the hope she'd understand.

'Can I undress you?' she asked.

'You can do whatever you want with me.'

She smiled and removed my T-shirt before moving to my trousers, then my boxers, until I stood before her stark naked.

'There,' she said, a smile wide on her face. 'Much better.'

'You like what you see?'

'Big time.' She ran her hands down my chest, her nails cutting into me, but not enough to break the skin. 'Now watch me.'

Madison reached behind her back and unhooked her bra with one hand. Her head tilted to the side, and her eyes gleamed with knowing. She enjoyed giving me a show as much as I enjoyed watching it.

She removed her bra, revealing her perky breasts and dusky hardened nipples.

Before I could close my jaw from its new position on the floor, she hooked the edges of her knickers with her thumbs, and at a tantalising pace, dragged them down her thighs to her feet until they were completely removed, and she was as naked as me.

'Come here.' She beckoned with her finger, and all I could do was follow her lead.

Madison got on the bed, and I did the same, lying down beside her.

My hand, unable to stay still, reached out to create

patterns on her stomach. Her hand appeared on top of mine and moved it down, down, down.

The bare skin soft beneath my fingertips changed, the heat of her core beckoning me.

'Are you sure?' I asked, hoping my constant questioning wasn't enough for her to stop this from happening.

'I'm sure,' she said, her face serene. 'Now stop asking and start doing. I want office Dylan, and I want him now.'

Office Dylan?

Ah, the image came to my mind in a montage. In my office, I had taken charge while also letting her stay in control.

I'd told her what I wanted, and I'd made it happen.

She'd liked that.

'Your wish is my command.'

Slowly, I pushed a finger inside her, her arousal so fucking wet and so fucking hot. A second finger. A lightning bolt of thrill ran through me when her back arched in response.

Watching Madison come undone was one of the best sights.

'Are you going to be a good girl?'

Her moan, her hissed *yes* nearly sent me over the edge, and she hadn't even touched me yet.

A third finger, almost too tight to fit.

'Dylan,' she breathed out. 'Dylan, don't stop.'

Well, one thing I did well was follow instructions.

My thumb joined in, stimulating the part where she wanted me, and her inner walls tensed.

'Fuck,' she moaned.

When she came down from the orgasm, I removed my

fingers and sucked the taste of her off them. She'd liked it when I did it in the office, and I could tell she liked it now. Her eyes were ablaze with a fire I never wanted to douse.

'Please,' she whispered. 'Please.'

Her pleas, the sound of her voice as she practically begged, fuck, it was the icing on the cake.

I placed my elbows on either side of her and came to rest above her, the head of my cock nudging at her entrance, wanting it as bad as me.

I wanted to ask again if she was sure, but something in her expression told me she knew I wanted to ask, so I stayed quiet.

A secretive smile softened her lips. 'I'm sure, Dill.'

It was enough to have my heart soaring, threatening to beat outside of my body.

I slid home, and fuck, it truly was heaven. The way she gripped me, the warmth of her, everything was perfection.

This, this was something I could get used to. Could never get enough of.

She moved her hands to rest on my hips, making it clear she wanted me to move.

So move I did.

We chose the pace together, one that had her moaning and me looking into her eyes and wondering how I'd kept my distance all this time.

Our eyes locked, and a lot passed in our gaze.

Things neither of us had said, but things we could both feel.

I reached between us so my thumb could stimulate her while I picked up the pace of my thrusting.

'Fuck,' I moaned out, the feeling of her tight heat clenched around my cock enough to have me seeing stars.

Madison fell apart.

Her moans, mixed with her tiny little breaths, had me coming undone.

Until we both crossed over the precipice together, our moans became a symphony I wanted to create again and again.

madison

Hand in hand, Dylan and I returned from our walk.

The sun, surprising for so early in April, shone down on us. I loved the way it warmed my skin. Any time I could leave the house without a coat on was a win in my eyes.

We were heading over to Dylan's parents' place for dinner and were already running a little late. Guessed that was what happened when you were enjoying yourself.

Since we'd had sex a couple of nights ago, everything had fallen into place between us. The barrier holding Dylan back was no longer there.

Sex with Dylan was everything I'd expected it to be—and some. Who knew he could have a dirty mouth when it suited? And who knew I'd love being called a good girl to the point I'd do things to make him say it again, and again?

My eyes glossed over at the thought of Dylan telling me to …

A piece of paper caught my eye, trapped in between the

window and the door frame on the passenger side of Dylan's car.

'That's odd,' I said, plucking it out of its wedged position and opening it up.

Dylan froze, his hand paused on the handle to open the driver's side door. 'What's that?'

'A note of some description. Maybe from my mum or the elusive Ralph,' I said. A logical enough explanation. Now I'd told Dylan about Mum, I didn't have to hide it from him anymore. And man, did that feel good.

'I'm on tenterhooks over here,' Dylan said, his tone light and jovial, but his eyes were anything but. 'What's it say?'

I read it in my head before handing it over to him.

> Madison,
> You should watch your back.
> You should watch where you're going.
> There are a lot of things you should do.
> The real question is, what will you do?
> One thing I know? You should be scared.

Dylan finished reading it and went still.

'You okay?' I whispered, worried whoever had left the note stood lying in wait somewhere, watching this all unfold.

'Of course I'm not fucking okay,' Dylan snapped, his eyes blazing. It made me wince, the anger there. The fear. 'I'm sorry, Mads. Let's get in the car.' He took a deep breath, his eyes darting around, looking for anything out of place. 'Remember to keep calm. If they are watching, they'll be looking for signs. They want you scared.'

With as much calm as I could muster, I opened the passenger door and got into the car, closing it with a small click behind me.

Once Dylan had got in, I said, 'I guess none of it has felt *real*. The case and whatnot. Even if my entire life has changed because of it.'

'I suppose this note makes it more real, doesn't it?'

'Well, yeah.' I shrugged. 'Do you think it could be from my mum?'

'There's no way to know for definite.' Dylan rubbed his jaw. 'It doesn't read the way my letters do.'

'That's what I thought. But it also feels a little too clever to be my mum.'

'Could be Ralph? Or the "bad people" she owes money to?'

'Hmm, true. I guess we'll have to stay alert and be on our guard.'

'Always.' Dylan locked his seatbelt into place and turned to me. 'Are you sure you're up for going to my parents' place for dinner?'

'The others won't be there, will they?' I asked, feeling like a coward for even asking. His siblings were my closest friends, but I wasn't in the mood to pretend in front of them.

If Bonnie had guessed about me and Dylan, then Mike knew too.

That made things simpler.

'Nope, just us two.'

'Okay, good.' The weight on my shoulders relaxed. 'Then yeah, of course I still wanna go.'

'Just remember, we can't tell them about this.' He placed

the note down on my lap, and I put it in the glove box, more than happy to forget about its existence. 'It'll only worry them more.'

'You know I'd never want to put your parents in danger. Not after everything they've done for me.'

'I know.' Dylan reached out and squeezed my hand briefly. 'And hopefully, one day soon, we can tell them a little more about all this shit. When it's safer.'

I nodded. 'At least we've got each other. I don't know what I'd do if I didn't have you to talk to.'

'It's you and me against it all, Mads.'

Dylan's response sent a shiver down my spine. You know, the real good kind.

dylan

MY ANGER TOWARDS THE NOTE MADISON HAD received the day before hadn't waned. If anything, it only grew more with each hour.

The two of us had sat through dinner with my parents as if nothing were the matter, as if the two of us weren't getting threatening letters and having to deal with shit people had no idea about.

One thing the entire ordeal had furthered was my skill of deceit.

Well, that, and my feelings for Madison Jones.

Even looking at her had my insides squirming—in a very good way, if such a thing existed. The way her eyes lit up when she smiled, the way she brushed her blonde hair away from her face whenever she experienced anxiety or uncertainty. All of it.

She'd sunk me, in a way Caroline never had.

Which told me everything.

On reflection, what Caroline and I shared had been

doomed from the start. She'd wanted something I couldn't give, even if I hadn't realised it at the time.

But things with Madison ...

They'd surprised me. Jumped up and made me take notice, regardless of what I wanted. Or of what I thought I wanted.

Working out at the gym always helped me clear my head, and knowing Madison was safe with Dawn at the office helped, too.

The more weight I added, the more reps I did, the better it made me feel. Purging the demons and dark thoughts.

Then there was the shit with her mum I still hadn't handled. Work and Madison took up all my time—not that I was complaining. How did you approach the mother of the girl you're-sort-of-dating-but-nothing's-official-yet and tell her to leave said girl alone?

Not that Jessa James would pay attention.

Yes, I told Madison she'd listen to me because of my lawyer status, but how truthful the statement was, I had no idea.

Didn't know where to find the woman, even.

Maybe one of my contacts in the Lakeland Police could help locate her.

Either way, Madison needed to be protected from all of those who wanted to harm her.

I finished my reps and sat back, breathing heavily, one question coming to me, demanding an answer.

Do people my age ask people to be their girlfriend?

It seemed juvenile, yet no alternative came to mind. Plus, with Madison being nineteen, maybe the terminology suited the situation in her eyes.

Only one way to find out.

———

'DAWN IS HONESTLY SUCH A SWEETIE. She told me we could visit her place in Spain whenever we could find the time, as long as it's free, of course.'

Madison's chipper voice filled the car, an incessant humming in the back of my mind mixing with it.

'Will you stop talking for a second?' I blurted, cutting her off.

She paused, her open mouth unsure what to do now it couldn't continue whatever it planned to say next.

Guilt washed over me.

'I'm so sorry, Mads. Ignore me.'

'You don't have to apologise. I get it. I watch how much stress you're under at work daily, then there's me chatting absolute crap while you try to drive. To be honest, I'm surprised you've not snapped at me before now.'

My stomach soured at the implication. 'That doesn't bode well for this relationship.'

'What doesn't?'

'The fact you expect me to snap at you. Says a lot.' My stomach soured. Did Madison think so little of me?

'No,' she said, reaching out her hand to touch mine. 'I didn't mean it like that. It came out wrong. I only meant you're dealing with a lot, and I'm doing nothing to help it.'

'None of this is your fault.' I took a deep breath, ready to say the thing on my mind, to let her in a little more. 'If it's anyone's fault, it's mine. Completely.'

'And you've come to that conclusion how?'

'It's the only logical conclusion.' I signalled to pull up at the next safe spot, not wanting to have to focus on the road while we spoke about something so important.

As soon as we were parked, I turned off the engine and faced her.

'I'm just so worried. All I want is for you to be safe, and I'm sorry for snapping at you. The note, along with everything else, has my anxiety spiking. If I hadn't rejected you, if I hadn't caused you to leave that night, then this wouldn't be happening.'

'You're right.'

'And I—' I stopped, her words catching up. 'Sorry, what?' I sputtered.

'I said you're right.' Madison smiled, her hand still on top of mine, rubbing small patterns absent-mindedly. 'If you hadn't rejected me, we wouldn't be here, in your car, heading to somewhere we're both calling home for the time being. We wouldn't be kissing, wouldn't be ...'

She trailed off, and the memory of our nights together flashed like my own personal movie montage.

'When we get home, maybe you could do the thing where you ...'

Her teeth teased her bottom lip. 'I'd like that.' She laughed. 'What I'm saying, Dill, is I'm happy we're here. Would I have rather not witnessed a murder? Duh! But I did, and it is what it is. We've made the most of it, and honestly, I'm totally okay with living in this timeline.'

The two of us had discussed different timelines a couple of weeks ago after watching a film where one event changed the course of the main characters' lives, and you followed along with both alternatives and watched how different the fallout from any situation could be. It opened my eyes a lot more than a fluffy romance normally did.

'There's no timeline in which this'—I gestured between us—'doesn't happen.'

A passing car's headlights lit her face, and once again, her beauty had me speechless.

'You okay?' she asked. The squeeze of her hand dragged me out of the depths.

'How about I call you my girlfriend and we be done with this casual dating malarkey?'

Her blue eyes sparkled. 'Only if I get to call you my boyfriend in return.'

dylan

WHEN DANA INVITED MADISON TO SPEND THE DAY with her at the library, I couldn't tell my sister the answer I wished to—a big fat no, she's fine thanks—and instead, had to agree it would be better for Madison if she could get away from me for a bit.

I had to laugh.

It would appear my family was attempting to put a spanner in the works of our relationship without even knowing there was a relationship to put a spanner into.

Thinking about it, what an odd saying. Probably British. Our language was filled with odd idioms.

On my way back to my office from the drinks station, Noah's head popped out of his door. 'Dylan, in here, please.'

I strolled inside to find Jeoff and Mick already in there, the two of them looking rather solemn. Mick scuffed the floor with the toe of his shoe, and Jeoff kept rubbing his rounded stomach in a circular motion.

'Everything okay?' I asked, coming to a stop before the three of them.

'Well,' Mick, seemingly at a loss for how to continue, faltered before mustering the words. 'It looks to me like we've got a problem.'

'A problem, sir?'

'A big problem,' Jeoff answered. 'From what we can gather, there's a rat.'

'A rat?' I was struck dumb, and apparently, could only repeat their words back to them rather than add anything worthwhile.

'A rat, a leak. Whatever you want to call it.' Mick picked up the trail. 'The Syndicate has somebody working under-cover in the force. Vital evidence has disappeared overnight.'

'Why would a cop do that?' I asked, feeling stupid the moment everybody turned their gazes to stare at me like I was missing a screw. 'Never mind, of course they'd do that. What kind of evidence?'

'Both the physical kind and the stuff being held on drives and the likes.' Mick waved his hand. 'What matters is the fact it's gone.'

'Shit.'

The three of them nodded at the expletive.

The past three years were on the verge of trickling down the drain, and my feelings were conflicted. On the one hand, it seemed inevitable the bad guys would somehow slither out of anything thrown at them. They were well known for being slippery bastards.

But also, a small part of me had hoped we'd get them. Show how justice always prevailed.

'So what happens now?' Noah asked.

'We tighten up the case against Malcolm,' I said. 'Not much else we can do.'

'And if the bastard pleads guilty?' Mick asked.

'We cross that bridge when we come to it,' I said decisively.

Jeoff winced. 'Let's hope Jaws doesn't get to Malcolm before this has the chance to go to trial.'

'You think he'd kill his own son?' I asked. To be fair, I wouldn't put it past him. Johnny 'Jaws' Silver was the head of The Syndicate and, by all means, not a nice man. You didn't rule an organisation like that for as long as he had without making enemies and evil decisions.

'I think the man would do a lot if it meant saving his own arse,' Mick said.

Noah and Jeoff nodded in agreement.

'It's a shame we can't get to the daughter,' Noah said, running his hand through his hair. 'Nobody knows where she is or who she is. Just up and disappeared into thin air twenty-eight years ago. She'd be forty-seven now.'

Mum's age. Knowing that made me glad she'd disappeared.

'If she's stayed gone for that long, then I wouldn't want to disturb her,' I said. 'Maybe we should be thankful she escaped that life.'

'Doesn't mean we can't hope the hard drive rears its ugly head,' Mick said, and Jeoff laughed. The hard drive that may or may not exist was a running joke in the office. 'She could at least mail it to the police anonymously.'

'We can only dream,' I said with a smile.

madison

FROM THE MOMENT DYLAN STEPPED THROUGH THE door, I could tell something was bothering him.

His usual happy demeanour was stolen from him somehow, and I didn't know how to handle it. Usually, Dylan's face lit up into a smile whenever he looked my way, but so far, he'd barely looked at me except for the perfunctory greeting he gave when he entered.

Even when I placed a plate of lasagne in front of him, his face stayed the same—and Dylan loved my homemade lasagne, a good thing really as it was pretty much the only thing I *could* cook. It had taken me ages, and I was super proud of it.

'Everything okay?' I asked once I took my seat next to him at the small two-seat dining table that we unfolded for meals, then hid again when not in use. 'Something happen at work?'

'Nothing for *you* to worry about.'

His emphasis cut right through me.

'Are you sure?' I asked, not knowing when to quit and shut up. 'I'm here to listen to whatever it is.'

'You don't understand,' he snapped. 'Everything's falling to shit.'

I blinked. He'd never looked at me with such anger before. An image of my dad's face came to mind, and I had to breathe out slowly, picturing my happy place instead.

Once I calmed down, I asked, 'Is there anything I can do to help?'

His patience with my questions disappeared in an instant. 'No, Madison. There's nothing you can do to make it better, okay? So stop asking stupid questions and eat your food.'

Shocked, I stared at him, unable to think straight.

I mumbled something about needing a drink. My legs threatened to buckle from underneath me on my way to the kitchen.

He'd never raised his voice at me.

Never made me feel so small, so insignificant.

It was like my parents all over again. They'd belittled me, told me I was useless, shouted at me, abused me mentally and physically.

And Dylan's reaction was enough to have the panic I pushed down come back to the surface.

My vision swam before me, black dots around the edges gaining on me. Getting closer and closer.

I couldn't breathe right. Couldn't see. Couldn't hear.

Everything hurt.

MAYBE IT WAS my breathing that alerted Dylan. Maybe it was the fact I'd crumbled to the kitchen floor, unable to keep myself upright any longer.

Either way, he came.

'Mads,' he called, rushing to my side from the table. 'Breathe, baby.'

I tried. Both to breathe and to tell him I was trying, but neither breath nor words came.

Why does nobody ever talk about the fact that panic attacks make you feel like you're gonna die?

Because that was the overriding thought in my brain. I would die and only a few people would care.

'Deep breath in through your nose, Mads. That's it, you can do it, baby. Then slow, exhale, out your mouth.'

I focused on Dylan's words. Followed his instructions and did the actions.

In through the nose.

Out through the mouth.

In through the nose.

Out through the mouth.

Slowly, my breathing became easier. My vision returned to normal.

And Dylan was crouched in front of me, worry bleeding out of every pore.

'I'm sorry.' He brushed the hair away from my face, tucking it behind my ear.

My bottom lip wobbled. The kind tone set me off, tears flowing thick. How could I explain the reason I'd panicked without having him pity me more than he already did?

'Let's get you to the sofa, yeah?'

I nodded, not ready to speak.

Dylan helped me to stand and then supported me over to the sofa. The softness of the cushions comforted me, cocooning me in their warmth.

'When you're ready to talk about ...' Dylan took a deep breath. 'I'm here for you, Mads. And when you're ready to talk about them, I'm here to listen.'

His lips brushed my hair, a soft gentle kiss placed on my head to help calm me down more.

'Raised voices take me back to a time I'd rather forget,' I whispered. Flashes of my parents' arguments came to me, but I batted them away before they could find purchase. They could no longer hurt me. 'You know my parents weren't the best people, especially when together.'

Dylan pulled me into a hug, the two of us finding a comfortable position together on the sofa automatically. Living with somebody and snuggling up every night had that effect.

He leaned in, kissed me, and I melted.

But even a kiss that could melt a frozen heart wasn't enough to keep the doubts at bay.

Maybe my forever crush on Dylan blinded me to some of his faults, and because of that, I overlooked potential red flags, not wanting to give them any credit.

If the evening was any indication, I couldn't overlook things anymore.

Were Dylan and me a good idea?

It was a question I needed to find an answer to before I lost my heart to him completely.

madison

'YOUR BIRTHDAY'S COMING UP.'

Dottie's reminder made me blink. Dottie always remembered my birthday without fail, even if she forgot a lot of other stuff.

'Oh, yeah. So it is.'

Time had flown since Dottie's birthday. Usually, time crawled by as if an age passed between the two events, but what with witnessing a murder and hooking up with Dylan, I hadn't thought much about my upcoming date of birth.

The only highlight of turning twenty? I'd no longer be a teenager and feel weird about being with somebody who'd turned thirty not too long ago.

Even if it was also a major turn-on.

Something I wouldn't tell anybody, even on pain of death.

'What we gonna do for it?' Dottie asked, plonking herself down on the Chesterfield.

'You know I don't care about celebrating my birthday the way you do.'

'I know, but let's at least go out for a meal or something. I hate to think you'll be here with only my smelly brother for company.'

Little did she know, her smelly brother made quite wonderful company. Actually, it happened to be the only company I wanted on my birthday.

But how to tell her that without actively telling her that? Hmm ...

'I suppose we could sort a dinner out,' I said, choosing to give in rather than stand up for myself.

Dottie may be my best friend, but now and then, I wondered if maybe I should stop enabling her.

Okay, maybe a little more than now and then.

'I'm gonna make a drink. You want anything?' I asked, needing to remove myself from the conversation for a moment. If one word described Dottie, it would be full-on.

'Please. I'm gonna pop to the loo.'

I nodded, preoccupied with getting the wine out of the fridge and finding some clean wine glasses.

She came back not long after, and I handed over her glass of wine.

'Wanna watch a film?' I asked, taking my place on the sofa, knowing she'd follow.

'Sure.'

AN HOUR LATER, Dottie spoke for the first time since the film started.

'This sofa is beautiful to look at, but I can't imagine it's nice to sleep on,' she announced, shuffling her bum to drive home her point.

It seemed silly to answer, seeing as I had no idea what sleeping on it would feel like, and neither did Dylan …

Did I feel like a right rotter for not telling Dottie the truth? A thousand times, yes.

Did it make me want to tell her? No. Not one bit.

The relief I'd get from telling her was far outweighed by the fall-out that would follow the revelation. For years, our friends or girls we went to school with had used Dottie to get closer to her brothers. In her eyes, I was the only one who never had and never would.

'How is Dylan finding it?' she said when I didn't answer. 'He's been staying here for like five weeks now.'

'Oh, er, I don't know.' My cheeks warmed. 'You'd have to ask him.'

She tilted her chin, sticking her nose up in the air. A sure sign she thought something was amiss.

'Are you not sick of him yet?' she said, a scowl settling on her lips. 'I think it's a bit bloody ridiculous that you didn't come and stay with us at the house instead. All of us would be there to protect you then.'

Honestly? The idea had never crossed my mind. I wondered if Dylan had thought of it and decided against it.

It's not like we could change it now. Not like I wanted to.

'It seemed silly to disrupt everybody. Plus, we'd have been on top of each other,' I said, pretending I'd thought of it before. 'I doubt it'll be for much longer.'

'My brother appears to have made himself at home here.'

'He does?' I filed through the cabinet of my brain to find

a reason she'd say that, but nothing apparent came to me. 'Better than him still feeling like an outsider, I guess.'

'Maybe.' Dottie's noncommittal shrug bothered me. Why was she acting so weird?

We fell back into silence and went back to watching the film, my previous relaxed state having disappeared.

I was on edge, waiting for the other shoe to drop.

A half-hour later, once the credits rolled, Dottie spoke up again.

'Since when did you start taking the pill?' She fidgeted until she got comfy again. 'Last time we spoke, you'd had no relations in months and hated messing your body up with unnecessary hormones.'

Ah, I had said that, like, two years ago. Not to mention taking the pill was a newer development.

Had she snooped through my bathroom cabinet, or had I left them out on the side?

Neither Dylan nor I wanted children, and the best solution was for me to take the pill until I could look into more long-term solutions.

'The doctor suggested it might help with my period pains,' I said, my tone bland even to my own ears. 'Thought I'd give it a try.'

'Makes sense.' Dottie looked at me dead on, and I found I couldn't look away. 'Mads, you'd tell me if something had changed in your life, right?'

'What do you mean?'

'Like if you had a boyfriend or something?'

I chuckled. 'You think I can hide stuff from you?' I waved her concern off, hoping she couldn't see right through me. A stupid hope, really, seeing as she always had in the past. 'No, I don't have a boyfriend.'

'You and I always tell each other everything.'

'Right ...'

'So I thought you'd tell me when you decided to fuck my brother.'

Her eyes blazed into mine, the heat emanating off them enough to burn me.

'I—'

'You what?' she seethed. 'You *forgot*?'

I tried again to speak, but she kept cutting me off.

'I cannot believe you! You're supposed to be my best friend, yet how can you be if you're willing to betray me like this?'

'I haven't betrayed you,' I said, wincing with each word, hearing it as a lie of sorts. Hadn't I told myself the whole time it was a betrayal of my friendship with Dot? 'If you'd let me explain—'

'No!' Dottie stood from the sofa, tears in her eyes. 'I don't want your explanation.'

'But I need you to understand—'

'Understand what? That you just lied to me when I asked about a boyfriend? That you've only stayed my friend all these years so you could fuck my brother?'

Every time she swore, I winced. Every time she said it, she reduced what Dylan and I shared together into something gross. Something wrong. *Twisted*.

'He's thirty, Madison! He deserves a woman his own age who isn't a scared, spineless cow.'

'Now wait a minute!' I said, moving to stand too. If I stayed sat on the sofa while she berated me, I'd only be acting like the scared, spineless cow she'd accused me of being. 'You're not being fair.'

'No, what isn't FAIR is that you've hidden something so important from me. That you could look me in the eye and lie to my face and tell me you're not seeing anybody or that you don't have a boyfriend.'

'Well, what was I meant to do?' I threw my arms up in despair. 'We knew you'd act like this.'

'WE?' If I thought she was angry before, well, her anger somehow reached a new higher level. 'You're that close you can speak for him now. Is that how it is?'

Dottie grabbed her coat from the hook and put her shoes on before stomping her way to the door.

The words she said next came out in a low, horrible tone she'd never used before. At least, not aimed at me.

'I am *never* talking to you again.' Her hand was poised on the front door. She opened it, about to flounce out of my flat, leaving me with no idea when I'd get to spend time with her next. I wanted to keep her there. Hold her back. Tell her not to leave. But I did nothing but stare at her, tears blurring my vision. I hated myself for never getting angry with Dot. For never sticking up for myself and telling her some home truths for once. 'You are dead to me, Madison Jones.'

dylan

CARILLO'S REALLY DID MAKE THE BEST BURGER IN the city, and I'd know because Noah and I had made our way through most places in our search for the best after-work indulgence.

'So come on,' Noah said after rubbing his mouth with a napkin. 'Fess up.'

'What do you want me to fess up about?'

'Don't be daft and act like you don't know.' He chuckled. 'You and Madison, of course. Something's going on there.'

'You sound pretty certain about that.'

'You spend all day every day with her.'

'So do you, technically. She's at the office with both of us.'

'Yeah, but I'm not spending my nights with her either.'

'I live with her,' I said, a smile on my face. 'Sort of makes being near her at night unavoidable.'

'Oh, and are you about to spout bullshit that you're still sleeping on the sofa?'

That caught me off guard. Not sure the two nights I spent on the sofa counted at this point. They were so far off in my memory I'd forgotten about them.

'That's what I thought.' Noah smirked, lifting his beer to his lips. 'So now we've established I know more than you think, why don't you fill in the gaps?'

'Not much to tell, honestly.' I rubbed my jaw, eyes travelling around the restaurant, having a nose, hoping to spot somebody famous. Ever since the actor Jackson James got photographed here, Carillo's had become a sort of celebrity hot spot. 'I asked her to be my girlfriend.'

'*Girl*friend feels appropriate for Madison, doesn't it, you cradle snatcher?' He laughed, but my stomach soured.

'Did you seriously just call me a cradle snatcher?' I shook my head, laughing along with Noah, my gut telling me others would only say much worse. 'She's twenty in like ten days' time.'

'I'm joking around. You know I like Madison. Me and Hallie have rooted for the two of you for a while now.'

'Yeah?'

He nodded. 'About time you two realised what we all did that first day she showed up at the office and you fell off your chair like an uncoordinated twat.'

'And what was that?'

'That you two are good together and clearly have strong feelings.'

A commotion at the door caught our attention. 'Who's that?'

Noah straightened his back in the booth, craning his neck to look at who'd entered.

'Looks like Parker Daniels and his wife just came in.'

Noah waved, but I didn't turn to look. Parker and his wife came to our table a moment later. 'Hey,' Noah said with a nod.

'Hey!' Parker's cousin, the actor Dahlia loved so much, lived in Noah's building, so we all knew each other enough to say hey to but not enough for anything too in depth. 'This is my wife, Atticus.'

The curvy, petite woman at his side smiled. 'Hey.' She tugged Parker's arm. 'Come on, P. There's a group of women over there staring at you like you're their next meal.'

'Ah, the ladies love me,' he said with no hint of irony. 'Have to catch up soon, you two.'

We nodded, and the two of them made their way to a booth hidden in the back.

'You ready to head out?' I asked, waving down our server to get the bill.

Time with Noah was fun and all, but I wanted to get home to my girl. She'd spent the day with Dottie, and I hoped my sister would be long gone by the time I got home. It was getting quite tedious to have to pretend to be platonic with Mads in front of Dottie, but the alternative meant telling her, and neither of us was ready for that shitstorm just yet.

Soon. We'd tell her soon. As a united front.

'You're rather eager to get home,' Noah said. 'Any particular reason?'

I chuckled. 'Oh, fuck off.'

Every time I unlocked the door with my key, a thrill ran through me.

The key symbolised more than being able to let myself into Madison's home, or at least in my mind, it did.

'Baby,' I called as I entered, not wanting to startle her if she hadn't heard the key turning in the lock, 'I'm home.'

She lounged on the sofa, her eyes closed, the TV playing faintly in the background, illuminating her face.

'Hey,' she mumbled, her eyes remaining shut.

I put my coat on a hook and kicked my shoes off into the rack. Going from the slight chill outside into the heated home had my blood rushing to the surface.

'You have a good day?' I asked. She murmured an undecipherable reply. I tried again. 'Everything okay?'

Madison's red-rimmed eyes peeled open slowly. Had she been crying?

She'd tell me if she had, right?

'It's fine.' She blinked away a tear. 'Everything's fine.'

Routine dictated Madison move over on the sofa so I could sit beside her, but she stayed put, her expression making me uneasy. Maybe her day with Dottie went awry, or …

'Did your mum show up? Or that bald guy?'

My question pulled her out of her funk. 'No. Why'd you think that?'

'Just trying to figure out what's going on,' I said, moving to stand next to the sofa, hoping she'd get the hint and move without me actually having to ask her.

Hmm, apparently not.

'Can I sit with you?'

She looked at her legs, then up at me, then back at her legs. 'Sure.'

When she moved her legs, I pounced on the spot, not wanting her to change her mind. Hugging her felt how I imagined hugging a stuffed toy would feel. I leaned in to kiss her lips, but she looked away, so my lips caught her cheek instead.

I'd acted shitty as of late, and it made sense she'd want to take a step back from me. From us.

'I think I'm gonna head to bed,' she said, her words robotic. 'It's been a long day.'

'We could watch something of your choice?' I'd suggest anything to make her stay and talk to me.

'Nah, I'm good. Watch something without me,' she said, standing up. 'I want an early night, that's all.'

'Want me to join you?' I asked, waggling my eyebrows, hoping to elicit some kind of reaction from her, like a smile or a small laugh, but nothing came.

She blinked down at me. 'I'm just shattered, Dill.'

I watched her walk away, wishing I could bridge the gap between us and delve into her brain to find out what was going on.

Wouldn't it be bloody typical for me to realise she was the perfect woman for me at the same time that she realised I was no good for her?

dylan

THE CONDENSATION ON MY PINT GLASS CAUGHT MY eye, and I watched as it trickled down the outside of the cool surface.

Dottie watched me with a hawk-like stare, and it unnerved me. I'd barely spoken all evening in fear I'd give something away to her about me and Mads.

Originally, I agreed to the dinner because Dahlia had said she'd be home, too, but apparently, somebody had a hair emergency she couldn't get out of.

'So,' Dottie said, placing her empty wine glass down on the glass-topped table. 'How are things at Madison's place?'

'Yeah, they're fine, thanks.'

'I was over there Sunday, and I don't know how you deal with sleeping on that sofa every night! Hard as rocks—that thing is after a couple of hours.'

'It's not that bad,' I mumbled. 'Guess I'm used to it now.'

To be fair, it probably wouldn't be the comfiest to sleep on, but it's not like I could tell her the truth.

'Guess so. You've been staying there a while now.'

'Yep.'

'What's it like living with somebody who's practically a sister?' Dottie laughed, refilling her glass with more rosé. 'As annoying as living with me?'

'I doubt that.'

'No, Madison is a lot nicer than me.'

No point in denying it. 'She genuinely is.'

Dottie's gaze pierced me from the opposite side of the table like she had a view straight into my soul. 'She told you about the date she's going on?'

The sip I took of my beer went down the wrong hole, and I choked, coughing and spluttering until I could get myself under control again.

Huh?

'What date who's going on?'

Dottie gave me a funny look. 'The date Madison's going on.'

'Madison's going on a date?' Could she detect the incredulity in my voice? Pure disbelief?

'Yeah, she didn't tell you about it?' Dottie shook her head, eyebrows raised high. 'Hallie and Dahlia set it up for her.'

'*Dahlia* did?' Why would Dahlia do that? I'd spoken to her about Madison. 'Why would she do that?'

'You got a problem with it?' Dottie's gaze only grew more suspicious every time I opened my mouth. 'I thought you'd be happy Mads had a date lined up. Not like she gets out much, is it? And if she got herself a boyfriend, you wouldn't have to play babysitter all day and night.'

'Who's the date with?'

'His name's Jason. Think he's a regular guy, not a model or anything like the guys Mads hangs around with for work. Pretty sure that's why Hallie chose him.'

Noah hadn't mentioned anything about setting up Mads on a date, and he and Hallie told each other everything.

'When did she agree to this?' I asked, wracking my brain to figure out when Mads last spent time with Hallie and Dahlia. She'd had her hair done, but that was ages ago, back before anything happened between us—before I saw the light and recognised how amazing she was.

'Think they suggested it when she got her hair done,' Dottie said, confirming my thoughts. 'But then she messaged Hallie while I was around on Sunday to ask for his number to set it up.'

None of it made sense.

Yes, Madison had taken a step back from me since I returned home on Sunday, but surely she hadn't arranged a date.

I'd acted poorly towards her in the last week, but was it enough to make her want to end things with me?

Had I fucked things up that spectacularly?

By the time I returned home, Madison had already taken herself to bed.

I went through the motions, got myself ready for bed, and found her still awake, staring up at the ceiling.

'Hey,' I said, pulling back the cover on my side and getting into its warmth. 'Tired?'

'Mhm,' she said, her gaze staying on the ceiling.

'Did you have a good night?' I'd invited her to come and visit Dottie with me, but she'd already made plans with my parents.

'Yeah. Your mum made macaroni cheese.' She smiled, the scar on her lip visible in the dimmed bedroom lighting. I'd asked her once how she got it, but she clammed up. 'How's Dottie?'

'Same as always. Spoke mostly about herself.'

Mads hummed, as if to say, *I know exactly what you mean.*

I lay down, copying Mads by staring up at the ceiling rather than looking at her, even if I wanted to look at her more than anything.

'Anything exciting happen at Mum's?'

'Nope. Your dad told me he'd help me learn to drive if I wanted.'

'That's nice of him. What did you say?'

'I said I'd rather never drive a death trap, and I'm happy muddling through this life as a non-driver.'

I laughed. 'I forgot how much you don't like the idea of driving.'

'It's never appealed to me. Lucky for me, I've got you to chauffeur me around.'

Her words were jovial, but I could sense a layer of something else lurking under the surface.

'Are we okay?' I asked. My eyes stayed on the ceiling. I didn't want to watch her initial reaction—or any reaction— to my question.

She took a while to reply.

'Yeah, I'm just all out of sorts. I promise to tell you when

I'm ready if you don't mind waiting?' She shuffled onto her side with her back to me. Since Sunday, she hadn't hugged me in the night or fallen asleep wrapped up in my arms. 'Goodnight, Dill.'

'Night.'

Doubt settled in the bottom of my stomach, a lead weight threatening to drag me down into the dirt.

When she was ready to talk, we needed to talk about it all. About Jason, telling Dottie, and finally, where we both stood in regard to how we felt towards each other.

dylan

THE DOWNSIDE TO WICKER GARDEN FURNITURE was that when you wore shorts, it left an imprint on your skin, and it got sort of uncomfortable after the first hour.

But Mum's pride in the furniture made me think twice before complaining.

The garden, her pride and joy, had been transformed since the last time I came over.

Mum and Dad's thirtieth wedding anniversary fell on the thirteenth of May, and they were throwing a garden party to celebrate.

Because it faced the south, the garden always caught the sun and, in the evening, glowed a gorgeous orange.

Dad had insisted we eat outside. *'Eating tapas outside feels right. Like we're in the Mediterranean.'*

It seemed foolish to point out that we'd never actually been to the Mediterranean. At least not since they had me, and whenever we asked questions about their time as a couple before us kids came along, they gave vague answers.

'Madison mentioned you offered her driving lessons,' I

told Dad, turning the conversation to the topic I cared about most.

Dad chuckled. 'The girl looked positively terrified. Don't think she'll be taking me up on the offer.'

I joined in with his laughter. 'No, I don't think so either.'

'I suppose she doesn't need to drive with you around.' Mum's words, although said with kindness, had the opposite effect. A knot formed inside me.

'Suppose not.'

'What's going on?' Mum asked. 'Have Madison and Dottie had a falling out?'

'What makes you ask that?'

'Well, Madison came here for dinner with us instead of going to Dottie's with you.'

'She said your plans were already in place.'

'They were, but she knows we wouldn't have minded her cancelling to join you.'

'I don't know.' I shrugged. 'Neither of them has said anything to me if they have.'

'I'm sure whatever it is will sort itself out.' Mum rubbed my hand before sitting back in her wicker chair, the sun shining on her face. 'How are things between you and Madison?'

'Oh, err ...' I trailed off, looking up at the sun and closing my eyes, enjoying its light on my skin. 'It's complicated.'

'Complicated?' Dad's gruff voice made me smile. Mike Winters found it hard to understand affairs of the heart. To him, love was simple. If you loved somebody, and they loved you back, then you made it work, regardless of whatever life hurled at you.

If you were meant to be, then the universe would make it happen.

'I can tell something's wrong, darling.' Mum's voice softened. 'Talk to us. We're always here to listen.'

'I don't know what's happened. One second, we were good, then I came home last Sunday from my dinner with Noah to find Madison acting super standoffish. Ever since, she's kept herself at a distance. Said she'll talk to me about it when she's ready.'

'Are you sure you haven't done anything to cause her to step off?'

'Nice to know the two of you have faith in me,' I grumbled. 'I acted a bit of a dick last week, but I thought we'd spoken about it and moved past it.'

'Why don't you start from the beginning?' Mum asked, and on impulse, I told her. It all spilled out. About the case. The Syndicate. The threatening letters. All of it.

With each new thing, their facial expressions grew more and more worried.

'... and then Jessa showed up, and the rage that consumed me at seeing her scare Madison. Well, it told me how much I cared about her. How much I wanted to resolve all her problems.'

Note to self: must find and speak to Jessa Jones before she comes around to threaten Madison again.

It had slipped my mind since entering my loved-up Madison bubble.

'Jessa?' Mum repeated. 'I didn't think that nasty woman knew Mads's whereabouts.'

'She's shown up twice now. Talking to her is on my to-do list.'

'Just don't get hurt,' Dad said. 'Not that I think Jessa will hurt you, but she knows a lot of people who could hurt you, or worse.'

I nodded because it was the truth. If Jessa owed ten grand to some bad people, then she knew some bad people who could kill me and hide my body in the blink of an eye.

'Whatever is happening, you and Madison will sort it out, sweetheart, but the only way to do that is to talk it out.' Mum rubbed the back of my hand in what I assumed she meant as a comforting gesture. 'We love Madison, and it's made us so happy seeing the two of you together.'

Mum was right. We needed to talk.

Because if the conversation with my parents had led me to any conclusion, it was this: I loved Madison Jones and wanted to make a life with her.

When I looked ahead to my future, it included her.

I got my phone out of my pocket and sent Mads a message.

> Hey, you. Hope you're having a good day with the girls. Can't wait to see you tonight x

madison

DOTTIE DIDN'T SHOW UP FOR GIRLS' DAY.

Her vow to never talk to me again was in full effect.

'Dahlia sends her regrets,' Dana said from the lounger next to mine. She was lying there, a book firmly gripped in one hand, a small smile on her face. 'Apparently, she got called in for an emergency in the city. Super top secret. Couldn't even tell me what or who it was for.'

'That does sound supersecret,' I said. 'Must be for Dahlia to miss a spa day.'

'True.' Dana placed her bookmark in her book and put it down on her lap. 'Dottie tell you why she's not coming? She didn't give a reason when I asked.'

Nope, nothing other than telling me I was dead to her.

'Nope. Maybe her schedule clashed and she didn't want to admit she'd put her work before us again.'

'Most likely. That girl forgets those who love her easier than she should.'

That was for damn sure.

I relaxed a little. With the awkward talk of Dottie out of the way, I could pretend everything was fine in my life.

If it were Dahlia lounging beside me, I would open up, fill her in on everything going on, and ask her opinion. But Dana was the Winters sibling I spent the least amount of time with, the one I didn't know how to confide in, and I worried if I told her, she'd side with Dottie and hate me, too.

'How's work going?' I asked Dana, hoping to get her started on a rant about Isaac that lasted long enough she'd forget to ask about me and my life.

It worked.

Dana groaned, loudly. Lucky for us, the pool area at the spa was quiet, and nobody else was within earshot.

'Don't even talk to me about that good-for-nothing waste of space.'

'What's he done now?' I laughed, imagining it to be something small. When I worked with the two of them that day, sparks were flying between them—and not ones of hatred or dislike.

'What hasn't he done would be a much better question.' Dana sucked her teeth.

I half listened for the next hour as Dana waxed lyrical about how much Isaac Wilson bothered her.

My mind wandered.

Things with Dylan since Dottie came over were a mess.

Part of me wanted to tell him. Let him know what had happened and let him decide whether he wanted me more than he wanted to hurt his sister.

But that same part told me not to. Because what if he chose Dottie? I couldn't handle the rejection. Not after things had actually happened between us.

Not now I know the taste of him. The way he looked in the morning.

The way his eyes lit up when he finished.

The way he whispered my name as I came apart.

Basically, coward, thy name is Madison.

At the end of the day, while we changed, I received a text from Dylan, and my heart sank.

> Hey, you. Hope you're having a good day with the girls. I'll see you soon x

'HOW WAS YOUR DAY?' Dylan asked the moment I stepped through the door.

'Okay,' I said, kicking off my shoes. 'Only Dana and I went in the end.'

'Was it nice?'

'Yeah, actually. Was good to spend time with her without Dottie or Dahlia dominating the conversation.'

'I can imagine.' Dylan chuckled, stepping forwards to hug me, but I diverted myself before he could. He ended up grabbing the air instead.

His eyes, filled with questions, tracked me as I made my way to the kitchen and got a glass.

'Mads,' he said, his tone sombre. 'I think it's time we have a talk, isn't it?'

I gulped the ice-cold water in my glass so I didn't have to answer straight away.

It sounded awfully like he was about to end things with me, and I wasn't sure I could handle it if he did.

Everything in my head was so jumbled.

I wanted Dottie back in my life, but I also didn't want to lose Dylan either.

There had to be a timeline where I could keep them both.

Dylan watched me from the living area, and I stayed put by the kitchen counter.

The physical distance between us was nowhere near as large as the one between us mentally.

'I know about Jason.'

Jason?

I stared at Dylan blankly, hoping that if I continued to stand and blink, he'd explain.

He didn't.

He just stood and blinked back.

'Jason?' I asked. My empty glass made a clinking sound when I placed it down on the counter. I regretted it the moment I did it, though, because it meant I no longer had anything to do with my hands to occupy them.

'The guy Hallie set you up with.'

Ohhhh, that Jason!

'Oh,' was all I said, lost for anything else to say.

'And I know you agreed back before anything happened with us, but I also know you haven't put a stop to it either.'

No, you stupid man, because I totally forgot about it. Neither Dahlia nor Hallie had mentioned it since. Was Jason even real, or was he a ruse for me to realise how I felt about Dylan? With Dahlia, I couldn't be certain.

Dylan continued, not leaving any room for me to speak. 'I'm gonna be honest with you, Mads.' He swallowed. My eyes caught on his Adam's apple, and a deepening sense of dread came to me. 'I don't want to be messed around, espe-cially now I'm falling for you.'

Falling for me?

Like falling *in love* with me?

Unable to hear my inner turmoil, Dylan kept talking as if his words hadn't changed me so thoroughly that I wanted to bathe in them.

'I think we need to take a break and put a stopper in this, just for a little while. I'm gonna give you some space and stay away for a bit, too.'

My mouth fell open.

I'd acted stand-offish since my showdown with Dottie, but it hadn't occurred to me that Dylan might leave before I sorted out how to deal with it in my head.

'B-but I want to be with you.' I took a deep breath, ready to tell him. *Inhale. Exhale.* 'Dot knows about us. She realised when she was here the other day, and I've been trying to figure out how to tell you.' I sobbed, my heart breaking. 'She told me she never wants to talk to me again.'

'Shit, I'm sorry,' he said. 'I know how much she means to you.'

Tears poured down my face. 'You mean more.'

He blinked. 'I—' He stopped talking and rubbed his jaw, and I swore his eyes were looking into my soul. 'I'm so sorry that we didn't get a chance to tell Dot in a better way, but I think it's best we cool it for a bit. Make sure this is truly what you want before we both blow up our lives.'

'Dill, please,' I whispered.

He took a step closer to me, his hand reaching out to brush my hair back behind my ear. 'I really care about you, Mads.' He pulled me into a hug. 'Everything's just gone full speed, you know? I'm gonna pack a bag and see if I can crash at Noah's for a couple of nights. Give us both some space.'

'But what about the bad people?' I asked. 'What about my mum?'

'I'll talk to the police, see about a watch. I'll talk to Mum about you working at the lanes so you don't have to come into the office.'

A shooting pain stabbed at my chest.

I zoned out while he put a bag together, rang the police, and then Bonnie.

My heart broke, shattering into a million pieces, and I could barely hold myself together. Could barely breathe.

When he was done packing, Dylan came and placed a kiss on my forehead. 'We'll talk soon, okay?'

I nodded, unable to speak.

Dylan left the flat, bag in hand.

And I crumbled, crying, with nobody to blame but myself.

dylan

I'D MADE MANY MISTAKES IN MY LIFE.

Yet my newest one put all the others in the shade.

On the night I left Madison's place, I'd gone to hug her, and she diverted away from me. Physically stepped out of my reach and headed to the kitchen to get away from me.

It was that moment, standing and grabbing thin air, it hit me—she was hiding something from me. Or maybe she didn't want me anymore and didn't know how to voice it.

I'd fallen for her, truly madly fallen, and if the feeling wasn't mutual, I needed to keep my distance for a bit.

At least until Madison voiced what she wanted. Told me what she felt.

The bombshell that Dottie knew about the two of us and she'd not told me, gutted me. I'd spent time with Dottie after that, who had also said nothing.

Well, not exactly. Dottie told me about Jason, clearly as a way to spite Madison.

Everything was fucked, and I needed space from it all. I

kept hoping I'd hear from Madison, but two days had passed since I left, and she'd gone radio silent.

Not a peep from her whatsoever.

So I decided to do what I did best: I threw myself into work.

A knock at the office door had me lifting my head from the paperwork in front of me. The anonymous letters had blurred after the tenth re-read, still making as little sense as they did the day they arrived. Nothing in their contents gave anything away about the writer, no matter how many times I read them.

Noah popped his head through the door. 'Can I come in?'

I gave a terse nod of my head. 'Sure.'

He shut the door behind him and locked it. I sat up straighter in my chair. 'Everything okay?'

'Think I should be asking you that, mate.' Noah took a seat in the empty chair on the other side of my desk. 'Not gonna lie, but I'm worried about you.'

'Worried about me?' I shook my head, hoping to shake off his worry with it. 'Nah, no need.'

'Gonna tell me what's going on, or do I need to drag it out of you?'

'Not much to tell.'

He glared at me.

'Okay, maybe there's something to tell, but it isn't that important.' I wondered if the lie was as loud and clear to him. 'Madison and I fell out the other night.'

'What happened?' He clasped his hands together underneath his chin, his elbows resting on the desk. 'Last we spoke at dinner, the two of you were blinding, then next thing I know, you're crashing in my spare room. Hallie's thrilled, as I'm sure you can imagine.'

I chuckled at that. Hallie and her pesky meddling were one of the reasons we were in this position—not that I told her that when she gave me the evil eye from across the living room of Noah's place.

It's not like I could go back to my place and stay with Dottie. She was at the bottom of the list of people I wanted to spend time with.

'That's what I thought, but when I got home, she acted so cold towards me.' Even a week later, I still couldn't wrap my head around the change in her. 'I gave it a couple of days, but it became clear something had changed in her feelings for me, so I left. Put us on a break.'

'You gonna talk to her?'

'Yeah, at some point.'

He tilted his head. 'It's clear you miss her.'

'Mhm.' Anything other than an agreement would be a blatant lie.

I hoped she'd message me soon.

I missed her so much it physically hurt.

madison

I MISSED DYLAN SO MUCH IT PHYSICALLY HURT.

A pain in my chest that didn't dissipate, no matter what I did or thought.

No message had come from him.

Not that I deserved it.

I'd acted like a shit to him, and the fact he'd put a break on things rather than ending our relationship told me I still had a chance if only I had the guts to reach out to him first. He had placed the ball in my court, so to speak. Yet every time I typed a message, my finger jabbed the delete button straight after.

It wasn't only Dylan I missed.

Dottie, a girl who always stuck to her guns, had stayed true to her vow so far. Knowing her, she'd stick to it until the day she died, regardless of whether she wanted to. Even if she realised she'd made a mistake, she'd never be the one to apologise first—to reach out first.

I mourned our friendship.

Why wasn't it spoken about more often? Friendships,

especially long-term ones like mine and Dot's, became a form of relationship in and of themselves. You had secrets, inside jokes, things only the two of you were privy to. Memories to last a lifetime. Then one day, poof, it was all gone. Nothing remained.

A death, of sorts.

So there I was, on my birthday, alone, with no plans and no messages, curled up on the sofa, feeling thoroughly sorry for myself.

A comfort film played in the background, one I could recite word for word—one I *was* reciting word for word. It only made me feel worse. Dottie and I had seen it at the cinema together when it was first released, back when we were barely teens.

The knock came at two-thirty.

Me, the delusional cow, thought maybe it'd be Dylan or Dottie or Bonnie or some other Winters standing there, arms open for a warm hug, a wide smile, and a present to boot.

Yeah, so ... not what happened.

Instead, Mum stood there, skeletal hands perched on her emaciated hips. Even her clothes, no doubt repelled by her, hung loosely, trying their best to get away.

'Happy birthday,' Mum said, her toothless smile unnerving. Something about a gummy smile put me on edge—even those given by babies. 'I'm so happy you're home.'

I bit the inside of my cheek, my eyes in search of the police officer who lurked watching my place. Mum, too oblivious to pay much attention to me, didn't bat an eye. Just stood there waiting patiently for me to reply.

'Not gonna invite me in?'

That snapped me out of my search. 'Why would I do that?'

'Wouldn't want your neighbours to spot me hanging around. Might get a bad impression of you.'

I hated how much her words sent a trickle of unease through me. I didn't like what it said about me. Whether I liked it or not, the straggly woman standing on my doorstep birthed me, and if that made people not like me, well, fuck 'em.

'I'd rather you stay where the neighbours can see you,' I said, standing taller.

'Tough shit,' Mum said, losing her patience with me. Her frail frame knocked me, and because it was the last thing I expected, the shock was enough for her to barge past me and gain access to my home. *Fuck*.

'I'm not leaving until you give me the money I'm owed.'

'How do *I* owe *you* money?' My laugh, filled with scorn, had her eyes narrowing. 'The moment I got a paper round at thirteen, you took half my earnings.'

She cackled. 'For food and rent and all the luxuries your father and I gave you.'

'Luxuries?' Seriously, did the woman even know the meaning of the word? 'I don't think eating noodles every day and living in a place without heating are classed as luxuries.'

'Depends on the country,' Mum said. The point was invalid, of course, but it wasn't like she'd ever understand that. In her eyes, she'd done all she could for me. Raised me. Gave me a roof over my head. The bare minimum that was expected of any parent.

'I don't have any money to give you. I'm out of work right now.'

'And that hotshot lawyer boyfriend of yours can't spare his future mother-in-law a few grand?' Her fingers twitched. Trust her to downplay how much money she needed. Her feet shuffled on the laminate flooring. Mum never could stay still. 'Have you told him about me?'

'Yes.'

'Where is he?' She looked around as if expecting Dylan to appear from behind the sofa. 'Poor Son. Nobody wants to be with you for your birthday, huh? Maybe if you weren't such a stingy bitch, people would want to spend time with you.'

I refrained from snapping at her, and for that, I deserved a medal.

Where were the police? I'd seen a couple of plain-clothed officers, spoke to one of them even, who watched my place day and night, but maybe they thought because I opened the door and didn't shout out, I wanted this person in my home. Probably should have given them a list with pictures.

Berating myself for not checking the peephole before opening the door would help nothing, but I'd do it anyway.

Idiot, idiot, idiot. You'd think I'd have learned by now.

During my inner breakdown, Mum had taken a step closer. Then another.

Until she stood directly in front of me.

For fuck's sake, Madison. Get your head in the game. My inner voice laughed. *Stellar pep talk.*

Mum flew at me, using my distraction as her in.

Her fist collided with the side of my jaw.

Where did she learn to punch like *that*? If I wasn't the one being hit, I'd sort of be a little in awe of her. The woman may look like the wind could blow her over, but apparently, she hid strength somewhere unseen.

'You.' *Punch.* 'Little.' *Punch.* 'Bitch!'

She knocked me off balance, and my head slammed to the floor. My vision doubled. Instead of one Mum, there were two. And both of them looked ready to kill.

Her attack intensified. She hid whatever she held in her hands, but she'd picked up an item that would do more damage than her fists ever could.

A pain, hard and fast, started in my stomach. My hand came away covered in blood.

I closed my eyes to the onslaught. *Please, let me disappear.*

The patch of blood beside me grew bigger and bigger. With each second that ticked by, it got larger. Bloody wonderful. A birthday bleed out.

My phone had landed beside me when I fell.

It lit up.

Dylan
Happy birthday, baby. I wish I could be with you to celebrate. I hate this distance between us, and I hope (but also don't), like me, that you're miserable. Dinner tonight? There's something important I need to tell you x

dylan

WHY DID I NEVER REALISE HOW BORING WORK could be before Madison?

Before she literally fell back into my life, I'd lived to work. It was the one thing that got me up each morning, the one thing I looked forwards to when I went to bed at night.

How fucking sad.

No wonder my family worried about me the way they did. They clearly thought I had a screw loose, and honestly, I was inclined to agree with them now that I'd seen the light.

And there I sat on Madison's twentieth birthday, in a boring meeting after putting us on a break like the bloody idiot everybody else had already figured I was.

Four days had passed since I last saw her beautiful face, and every single one had crushed my soul a little more. I missed her so much. I wanted to kiss her, hug her, tell her everything would be all right if she'd just talk to me. Open up. Tell me whatever she was keeping hidden.

Anything.

I got my phone out and typed a message, pressing send straight away so I didn't second-guess myself and delete it.

> Happy birthday, baby. I wish I could be with you to celebrate. I hate this distance between us, and I hope (but also don't), like me, that you're miserable. Dinner tonight? There's something important I need to tell you x

Sent.

Now the ball was once again placed firmly in her court.

The two ticks next to my message turned blue, meaning she'd read it.

I waited, hoping the top would change to *Madison is typing* ...

And I waited some more.

AN HOUR PASSED, and Madison still hadn't replied.

I suppose that told me all I needed to know. She didn't want to get dinner with me and most likely wanted to end things but didn't know how to tell me.

Wonderful.

Fucking wonderful.

If she still hadn't replied when I finished work, I'd call her or go over to her place with her gift and a card.

My self-imposed break from her caused me physical anguish, and I needed to see Madison's face to feel right again.

Mum had tried calling five minutes ago, but I wasn't in

the mood to talk to her. I wasn't in the mood to talk to anybody.

The work on my desk, untouched, glared at me. Absolutely no part of me cared about it. All my care had gone with Madison.

A banging came on my door, startling me from my melancholy.

'Dylan!' Dawn's voice, high and screeching naturally, even higher and screechier than normal. 'Dylan, are you in there?'

'Come in,' I called.

Dawn's terrified face had me standing up in a panic.

'Dawn, what is it?'

'It's Madison.' Her lower lip wobbled, and when I looked closer, the faint shimmer of tears in her eyes became apparent.

My heart sank. 'What about her? What happened?'

'She's in Lakeland Hospital,' Dawn said, flicking away a tear from her left eye. 'She's been badly beaten. Your mum called the desk, said you weren't answering your phone.'

On autopilot, I picked up my things and rushed from the office, not once looking back.

THE WAITING room was empty except for Mum.

'Dylan, darling.' She opened her arms wide, and I flew into them, not too tough to admit I needed a hug from my mum desperately. She'd know what to do to make it all better. She always did. 'Come, sit down. Let's talk.'

I plonked my bum into the bright-red plastic chair next to Mum's.

'What the fuck is going on?' I blurted out.

Mum looked about to admonish me for swearing but thought better of it. 'Jessa paid Madison a visit today.'

My stomach sank. The guilt, already there, only grew bigger with the news.

'Oh.' I rubbed my jaw, my mind rushing through too many things to latch on to anything to say. Nothing I said would make any of this better, so why try?

'The police didn't suspect anything when Jessa entered the flat as Madison opened the door and didn't act scared or say anything.'

'This is all my fault.'

'No, dear.' Mum grabbed my wrist and put her hand on mine. 'If we're going to sit here and play the blame game, then you should add my counter to the board.'

'What? Why?'

'I was running late to pick her up for her shift at the lanes. Your sister called me frantically about some silly thing, and I got distracted.'

'But on that basis, it could be Dottie's fault, too.'

'Exactly my point,' Mum said. 'So let's stop this fault business.'

'No, but it is my fault, Mum.' I took a deep breath, my shoulders fighting to rise against the weight upon them. 'I promised Madison I'd talk to Jessa and sort it out, but every time I remembered, something else happened, and I'd put it to the bottom of my to-do list.'

'That's life.' Mum smiled; her eyes glazed over a little. 'We all mean to do things, but time is a tricky bastard.'

Hearing Mum curse always made me smile. It only happened on rare occasions.

'She'll be okay, won't she?' I asked, unsure how bad Madison's injuries were. 'She's not—' I couldn't finish the thought.

'She's gonna be right as rain in a week or so. I'm not sure of all the details myself and won't be until Madison wakes up enough to tell me.'

Everything had gone wrong. This wasn't the birthday she deserved.

Madison deserved so much more than life gave her, and once she got better, I would do everything in my power to show her how much she truly deserved.

She was a princess—no, a queen—and fuck, I'd never let her forget it.

'Go home and get some rest.' Mum rubbed the back of my hand. I opened my mouth to protest, but Mum gave me *the look*, and whatever I planned to say died on my lips. 'I'll message you once I've spoken to her, okay?'

I nodded, dejected.

Then I left her there, beaten and bruised, broken with every step I took that put me further away from her.

madison

HOSPITAL SUCKED—OF COURSE IT DID, IT WAS THE hospital—and I hoped they'd let me go home soon because even after only three days I was ready to discharge myself.

Being alone meant my mind had time to wander—and wander it did.

My mum, Dylan, and Dottie—they all ran on a loop, each fighting for the forefront.

Dylan had come as soon as Dawn told him about me being admitted, but Bonnie had sent him home to rest and messaged him when I woke up.

I texted him to thank him for caring and to tell him I wasn't ready to see him yet. I didn't want him to see me in such a state.

He respected my wishes and stayed away, but every morning and every evening without fail, I received a swoon-worthy message from him.

Today's morning text read:

> Morning, beautiful. I miss your eyes. Your
> lips. Your face. But most of all, I miss
> you x

I missed him more than anything—more than I ever thought possible.

Bonnie had stayed by my side throughout visiting hours, and my love for her grew every hour. Her actions were those of unconditional love, a love my mother never learned.

Dottie's tentative knock at the door took me by surprise. 'Hey,' she said, uncertainty swimming in her gaze. 'Can I come in?'

Bonnie looked at me, letting me decide, and I nodded.

From what she said to me, I guessed Bonnie knew a lot more about the situation than she let on. I respected her for not prying.

Bonnie stood from the uncomfortable chair she'd claimed for her own and rubbed her hands on her trousers, a small smile on her face. 'I'll leave you two to talk while I go and grab myself a coffee. You want anything, Madison dear?'

'No, thank you.'

Bonnie looked at Dottie, who also mumbled a no.

'Okay, well, I'll be gone for a little while. Stretch my legs.'

Neither of us called her out for acting so transparently, but Dot and I caught each other's gaze, a smile playing on our lips.

The moment Bonnie had moved out of earshot, Dottie spoke.

'I am so, so, so sorry, Mads.'

'What for?' I laughed. 'It's not your fault I'm in here.'

'Not for that and you know it.' She frowned, unable to look at me. 'I'm sorry for what I said to you.'

'I—'

'No.' She cut me off from saying whatever appeasing thing came to mind. 'Stop making excuses for me and my shitty behaviour. I'm eighteen now and need to fess up to my own mistakes.'

Well, that told me.

'Let me get this out before I allow you to talk me out of it.' Dottie plonked herself down into the chair beside me, the plastic cushion squeaking in protest. Her gaze still hadn't met mine, instead remaining on her hands, wringing together. 'I'm sorry I said you were dead to me and that I never wanted to see you again. It was childish, and a lie, and so bloody stupid!'

I looked away from her.

A bird flew past the window, catching my eye. At least I had a window view while stuck in purgatory. Or was this hell?

I looked back towards Dottie. Not that I owed her my full attention, but I wanted to give it anyway. For me, not her.

'I didn't even give you a chance to explain yourself.' Dottie's head raised, her red-rimmed eyes taking me by surprise. It was a well-documented fact that Dottie usually faked an apology to get her own way, or to manipulate somebody into doing her bidding. This time, though, it didn't feel like a manipulation. 'And since speaking to Dahlia about it, it would appear I was the only one who didn't know about the chemistry between you and Dylan.' She laughed, mocking. 'And I always pride myself on being able to spot things people hide.'

A cloud of tension had entered the room with Dottie. It still lurked above us both, a little clearer but not quite gone.

'But that's not all I'm sorry for,' she continued, darting her hand out to grab mine. 'I'm sorry for telling Dylan about the date with Jason and making it sound like you still planned to go on it. That you'd told me about it personally the day I came over.' The day I took a step back from Dylan and put some distance between us. No wonder he assumed the break was something I wanted.

'So that's why he put us on a break, thinking he did the right thing,' I said, breaking my silence.

She nodded, the tears in her eyes threatening to spill over. 'I was so angry at you, and when he came over for dinner, I figured out you hadn't told him about me knowing, and I took advantage. It was vindictive and petty and bitchy, and I am so sorry for all of it.'

Not like I could deny it. Her actions were all of those things with bells on.

'I know this probably means shit to you right now, but I think you should talk to him and work it out. It's clear to everybody how into you he is—how in love with you he is.' Dottie locked eyes with me. 'I'm giving the two of you my blessing.'

I scoffed at the audacity. '*Your blessing*?' I took my hand out of hers. 'Funny enough, Dottie, the world doesn't revolve around you. I'd already decided to talk to him before you sauntered in here, thank you very much.' I sat up straighter in the bed.

Of course Dottie would think not having her blessing held me back from pursuing things with Dylan again. It would never even enter her mind that other reasons were holding us both back. This was the land of Dot, and even though she'd apologised, she still thought she existed as the centre of everything.

Not that I'd tell Dot this, or anybody for that matter, but just because I'd decided to sort things out with Dylan regardless of Dottie's feelings, didn't stop the elation from rushing through me at the knowledge she wasn't going to stand in our way. That she didn't hate me anymore.

Dottie, looking thoroughly cowed, mumbled another apology.

Another thing I hadn't voiced aloud? I wanted to be in Dylan's presence more than anything but not until I got home.

I didn't want him to come to me in the hospital and feel guilt or believe it was all his fault, causing him to make a decision he wouldn't otherwise.

No. It was best to wait it out and hope I got home soon.

dylan

EVERY DAY SINCE SHE WAS ADMITTED, I'D SENT Madison her favourite foods. It was universally acknowledged that hospital food wasn't the best, and nobody knew how long Madison would have to endure it.

Food. One of Madison's love languages.

Mum had stayed by her side the whole time, supporting her, and she sent me updates daily.

My messages to Madison, morning and night, were being read but not always replied to. She'd sent me a couple of messages since waking up: one to tell me not to visit as she didn't want me to see her in hospital, another to tell me she wanted to speak in person as soon as she got home.

Genius me thought a break would help, yet once again I was wrong. It probably wouldn't be the last time either.

My phone flashed, and I grabbed it, my heart beating a mile a minute.

The message from Mum sent said heartbeat plummeting.

Dottie has come to visit. Maybe you
should think about doing the same. xo

Even at the age of thirty, she could still admonish me without being anywhere near me and make me feel five again. It was a special skill of hers. One most mothers had, or so it was said.

I understood why Mum wanted me to visit. If anything, by staying away, it looked as if I didn't care for her at all, but that simply wasn't the truth.

Madison knew I'd be there in a heartbeat.

But she'd asked me not to, and I could respect her wishes.

What good would it do to force me into her space while she recovered in the hospital?

When Madison's ready, I'll be there x

It was the same reply I'd given any time she mentioned me coming to visit.

Before I talked to her, I needed to get rid of the guilt within me. If only I'd spoken to Jessa, the way I'd promised. Madison must feel so let down by me.

20/04

Hope you've had a good day, beautiful. I miss the way your lips curl at the edges when I say something funny. Which, I'll admit, is a rare occasion x

21/04

Morning, Mads. I would ask what your plans for the day are, but I'm certain they're the same as yesterday and the day before. I miss breathing in your scent. Yes, I know that makes me sound unhinged, but you'll have to tell me what perfume you use so I can spray my office with it and always be reminded of you x

Night, my heart. May your dreams be as sweet as you x

22/04

In my dream, you were beside me, your head resting on my chest. I miss it. I miss you x

Sleep well, baby. The moment you want me by your side, I'll be there x

23/04

Wish you were home, safe, and well. My heart hurts knowing you hurt x

You make my life better. You make ME better. Good night x

24/04

Madison, my days are grey without you, as you have taken the light x

My message this morning when read back reads like an accusation, which was never my intention. You haven't taken the light because you are the light. You are my light x

25/04

It has been too long since I kissed your face, saw your smile, heard your voice. I miss you more than you could ever know x

Mum said you're being discharged tomorrow, thank fuck. We never got to celebrate your birthday together, and I hope one day soon we can. There are so many things I want to say to you, but they can wait until you're better x

26/04

Happy return home day. I can't wait to see you. The moment you're ready, let me know, and I'll fly into your arms x

madison

DYLAN'S TEXTS GOT ME THROUGH THE DAYS.

Each one put a smile on my face and only made me miss him all the more.

After the first couple of days, I expected him to taper off and not bother with me anymore, but that said a lot more about me and my self-worth than it did Dylan.

The smile on my face threatened to split it wide open when his latest message came through.

> Happy return home day. I can't wait to see you. The moment you're ready, let me know, and I'll fly into your arms x

Bonnie eyed me from across the bed.

'What's got you smiling like the Cheshire Cat, huh?' The glint of mischief in her eyes told me she'd guessed at the answer.

To lie to her face would be silly. 'Dylan.'

Her smile grew wider at her oldest son's name.

'I hope you're going to talk to him soon and put me out of my misery.'

I scoffed at her dramatics. 'This been eating you up inside, Bon?'

'It has, dear. More than you know.' She looked so sincere it made me chuckle. 'You two are meant to be, and I'm getting rather old waiting for you to realise it.'

'Maybe I'll arrange something,' I said. 'It's not a certain, you hear?'

'Yes, yes.' Bonnie pottered around the room, tidying up my things and placing them into bags for me. 'You're an independent woman, I know.'

Dottie entered the room, or should I say, she stormed into the room with a swagger only she had the good fortune to possess. 'Who's an independent woman?'

I prodded my chest. 'Me, according to your mum.'

'Mum's right,' Dottie said with a decisive nod. 'You don't need anybody to make you whole. You're perfect as you are.'

Things with Dottie and me were back to how they were before, sort of. There was no way I'd let her dictate my life the way I had in the past, and if she changed her mind about being okay with me and Dylan, then tough tits. It wasn't up to her.

But she truly was my best friend. My other half. And I loved her despite her faults.

'Thanks. Quite the ringing endorsement coming from you, Dots.'

'I thought so,' Dottie said, with no ounce of sarcasm or joking in her voice. 'We ready to go? I've got an event at five, and I am nowhere near ready for the world to gaze at me.'

'It's not even midday,' I said, my tone flat.

'Madison, you're being obtuse on purpose. It's ten to twelve, so it practically *is* midday.'

'Dot, would it kill you to calm down?' I laughed, letting her know I was joking.

'Whatever! If I don't get to Amelia's place by two, I'll have to do my own hair, and you know I hate that.'

'I'm ready now,' I said, laughing at her theatrics. 'Just waiting for the nurse to come and hand me my discharge papers.'

***

MY FLAT LOOKED COMPLETELY different from how I left it.

Not that I'd made a note of everything out of place before the ambulance arrived, but there was no way my mum and I left it looking so immaculate.

Every surface gleamed.

The kitchen counter practically shone if you stood at the right angle, and the light bounced off my fridge door's reflective surface—something rare but strangely beautiful.

'What the?' I asked, nervous to even put my house key down in case I made the place look untidy and unravelled all the cleanliness back to its former state.

On autopilot, I went to the cupboard and pulled out a glass.

Filled it with ice and water.

Then leaned back by the sink to look out into my living area.

The throw blanket I'd tossed aside when Mum knocked was folded neatly, resting on the arm of the sofa.

'Thank you so much for this, you two,' I said, finally taking my eyes off my tidy home to Bonnie and Dot, who were watching me closely. Not sure if they expected tears or horror, but apparently, my thanking them wasn't anticipated. Bonnie smiled, and Dottie frowned.

'Why are you thanking us?' Dottie's frown deepened.

I stared back blankly. 'For tidying up ...'

'The fridge is stocked and the cupboards too, dear,' said Bonnie, her smile widening. 'Think you'll even find there's a homemade cheesy cauliflower and broccoli pasta bake ready to heat up.'

Cheesy cauliflower and broccoli pasta bake?

Only one person made that to my satisfaction.

Bonnie's smug face made sense.

'Dylan did all this?' I gestured around the room, somehow hoping to encompass all I meant with it.

'He still has a key,' Dottie said, her frown altered into a grimace, probably worried I should've stayed in the hospital a little longer, or whether I had any lasting damage causing me to act so thick.

Nope, just apparently my self-worth lived on the floor, not to mention my belief in Dylan and how much he cared for me.

'So he does.'

The realisation caused a rush of longing and love my way. Even while I ignored his messages, he continued sending them. Even knowing I hadn't agreed to spend time with him yet, he'd made the effort to tidy my home the way he knew I liked, had filled my cupboard and fridge with my favourite foods, not to mention all the food he had delivered to me while I stayed in the hospital.

Fuck.

I'd made a right mess of it all by ignoring what existed between us.

My message thread with him was still open on my phone.

> Thank you so much for tidying and going shopping for me. I appreciate it more than you know.

> And thank you for your messages. Whenever I had a low moment, I reread them, happy in the knowledge you were thinking about me as much as I was thinking about you.

> I hope you're ready to fly.

'The smile on your face better be because you messaged him finally and not because of some ridiculous me-me.' Bonnie crossed her arms, her stern expression enough to make me and Dottie burst into giggles.

'Me-me?' Dottie repeated, struggling to repeat the phrase through her laughter. 'What the heck is a me-me?'

Bonnie laughed, too. 'Oh, you know. One of those picture things.'

'A *meme*,' Dottie emphasised.

'Yes, one of them.' Bonnie smiled, nothing phasing her. The woman rarely got embarrassed, even when she got social media things wrong. 'You girls and this modern stuff.' She pointed at me. 'Did you text Dylan?'

I thought about denying it just to mess with her a little, but the hope in Bonnie's eyes had me spilling all.

'Yes.' My cheeks warmed with a blush. 'Bowling this Sunday, right?'

'Don't you even think about it,' Bonnie said, wagging the finger still pointed at me. 'I want you here and resting.'

I groaned. 'But all I've done is rest.'

'Madison Isabella Jones.'

Ah, Bonnie was full-naming me. A sign she meant business.

'Yes.' The word sounded petulant. My pouting bottom lip probably didn't help with that image.

'If your bum is found in the lanes at any time before I give you permission, I will not be a happy bunny. Do you understand?'

Dottie laughed from the sofa. Trust her to get comfortable for the show. 'Yeah, Mads. Listen to Mother.'

'Fine!' Easier to accept it than to fight. 'I'll stay home all weekend on my Jack Jones and be bored out of my brain.'

Bonnie's smile was smug. 'You do that, dear.'

dylan

MUM TOLD ME THE MOMENT I ARRIVED AT THE alley that Madison wasn't coming.

I'd already guessed, but having it confirmed made me sad. I missed seeing her face, but also, who else could I get so competitive with?

The entire night didn't feel right without her there.

Since I received her message the previous day, we'd been communicating non-stop. We'd arranged dinner for the next night.

I was counting down the hours.

My phone buzzed.

Beat them all! x

Would rather beat you x

How dare you! I've just got out of hospital. One beating was enough, thank you very much x

I rolled my eyes at her response. She knew what I meant. Though having her joke about it was better than having her crumble.

> Very funny. You deserve a medal for comedic genius x

> I do. I suggest you get started on it the moment you get home x

> Your wish is my command x

'What's got you smiling so wide, huh?' Dottie asked, coming to stand beside me. Her signature perfume, something she swore she'd never change, tickled my nostrils. 'Madison, by any chance?'

I blinked, surprised.

'Err ...' I shuffled, cancelled out of our conversation, and put my phone back in my pocket.

'You don't have to lie to me,' Dottie said, a smile on her face. 'I owe you an apology.'

'An apology?'

Dottie took in a deep breath, her hands fidgeting at her sides, a sure sign of the guilt eating away at her about something. 'Okay, so hear me out first before you fly off the handle.'

I stared at her, my gut telling me whatever she had to say wasn't going to be fun to hear.

'So you know I spent the Sunday with Mads while you had dinner with Noah?' I nodded. 'Well, there were some things in the bathroom and her bedroom that made me suspicious about you two. So I dropped hints. Waited for

Mads to fess up and tell me the truth. But she didn't. She lied to my face, told me she didn't have a boyfriend.' Dottie paused, her former anger lingering on her features. 'And I just saw red. I couldn't believe she'd hide something like this from me. You, I'd expect it from, but not Madison.

'So I confronted her. Wouldn't let her explain. I said ...'—her eyes misted with tears—'I said some pretty awful things to her. Then I left.'

Ah, it all added up. The night I'd got home and she'd taken both a physical and metaphorical step back from me, from us, was all because of Dottie.

My fingers twitched in my pocket, the only sign of my anger, and I watched my sister. Yes, Dottie felt bad and right-fully so, but my forgiveness all depended on *why* she felt bad.

She continued, 'When you came over for dinner a few days later, it became clear she hadn't told you, so I mentioned the whole Jason thing to spite you both. She never asked for his number, and she never had any intention of going on the date. Madison never even told me about the date, not once. I was so angry at you both.'

I had to admit to myself, even though I would fight for Madison anyway, it was good to know for certain she'd never intended to date another guy. That she didn't ask for his number or tell Dottie about the date.

'How did you find out about the date thing?' I asked.

'Ah,' Dahlia said, joining us. 'That would be because of me.'

I turned to look at the sister who usually had my back.

Dahlia sighed. 'I knew you two liked each other, but for some reason'—she glared at me, the implication clear

—'nothing was happening. So me and Hallie devised a plan to give you both a little ... nudge.'

My lip curled into some semblance of a smile. 'A nudge?'

'You two were taking forever!' Dahlia's look of disapproval set me off, and I had to chuckle at her ire. 'Something had to be done about it.'

'All right,' I said, throwing my hands up to pacify her. 'I get why you stuck your nose in and arranged the date.' I turned to Dottie. 'But I don't like how you twisted it to hurt me.'

'I am so sorry, Dill.' Her bottom lip jutted out into a pout. 'I promise you, I'll never get involved in your relationship ever again.'

'Right now, I'm not sure there's a relationship for you to get involved in.' The words came out in a sulk.

'Oh, hush up,' Dahlia said. 'The two of you will sort this out, and you'll be back to your nauseating selves in no time.'

'We aren't nauseating.' I crossed my arms across my chest. 'We're cute.'

'You keep telling yourself that, sunshine.' Dahlia shook her head. 'I best be off to make sure Dana isn't killing us with her cocktails. That girl doesn't understand measures.'

With that, she headed off to Dana at the bar, who did look to be making up the contents of the glasses in front of her with little knowledge of the how.

'Dill, do you forgive me?' Dottie said, breaking the silence.

'Of course, but don't pull anything like that ever again, you understand? You're not a child anymore, Dot. Your actions have real-life consequences.'

She nodded, chastised. The two of us hugged it out.

'I'm sure you're gonna say the same as Mads, but for what it's worth, you've got my blessing,' said Dottie when I let her go from my embrace.

That had my ears pricking up. 'Why? What did Mads say?'

Dottie laughed. 'She totally called me out on my shit. Told me she didn't need my blessing and had already decided she was gonna talk to you.'

'Good. I'm glad Madison stuck up for herself against you.'

Dottie nodded. 'Yeah, I've been a pretty poor friend to her, but I'm gonna do better. Be better. Dottie version two point oh.'

'I'll believe it when I see it,' I said with a laugh.

Happiness coursed through me, my body and spirit lighter than when I stepped into the bowling alley.

I looked at my phone. Madison had replied.

You can bring it with you tomorrow

Only one more sleep to go!

I can't wait to see your face x

dylan

Nerves filled my stomach, bubbling away in there like it was their business to make themselves known.

Madison's door loomed in front of me, beckoning me forwards from where I still stood beside my car. I needed to find the courage to take the first step.

Our messages were flirty and filled with banter, but none of them had been about anything deep deep. Neither of us had touched on anything about *us*.

Here goes nothing.

I pressed the lock on my car, waited for the beep, then headed to Mads's door and knocked.

'It's me,' I said. Yes, she expected me, but I also didn't want her scared to answer in case somebody else had shown up uninvited.

'Hey,' she said, opening the door wide enough for me to enter. 'Thanks for coming.'

So proper and formal, I almost laughed. Almost.

I walked over to the sofa and sat, and Madison closed the door behind me with a soft click. 'How come you didn't let yourself in?' she asked, curiosity in her tone. 'I know you've still got your key.' Her warm smile had me sending one back. 'Thank you for what you did while I was in hospital. The food, the tidying. I appreciate it so much.'

'It was nothing.' I waved it off because it truly was nothing. She deserved it, and more. 'And I didn't want to presume anything by letting myself in.'

'Thanks for saying it was you,' she said, sitting down on the sofa beside me. 'I've been thinking about getting one of those video doorbells. It'd be good to have footage, wouldn't it, if anything happens?'

'Good idea.'

A lull came, neither of us sure how to fill it.

Did we jump straight into it? Or did we need to navigate it like a rocky terrain with potholes?

'Did you want a drink?' Mads asked.

'I'm okay, thank you.'

I twiddled my thumbs. She adjusted her position.

The stupidity of our actions wasn't lost on me, but how to break it?

Maybe the best line of attack was to just ... put it all out there.

'I love you,' I blurted, with no finesse whatsoever.

Madison studied me, hope in her gaze.

'I love you, Madison Jones,' I repeated, with more conviction this time. 'You make my life better, and I hated spending time apart from you. Silly me thought it was what you wanted, and instead of talking to you about it, I made the decision for us.' My actions still pissed me off, but they were in the past, and I needed to move on from them and forgive myself. 'I'm an idiot of the highest measure. I hope you can forgive me.'

Her reaction was unexpected. She laughed, the chuckle nearly sending me over the ledge, my thoughts spiralling. What did she mean by it?

'Don't be so hard on yourself, Dill.' She smiled, her hand reaching out for mine. I took it, bringing it to rest on my knee. 'There's nothing to forgive. I made some pretty stupid decisions, too.' Her eyelashes fluttered against her cheek. 'If I'd just spoken to you about Dottie finding out instead of hiding and curling up into a ball inside myself, then things would've been different.'

'It's in the past; there's no point us dwelling on it.'

'No, you're right,' she said. 'But talking about it and dwelling on it aren't the same thing.'

'That's true. Why didn't you tell me before you felt backed into a corner?'

'I was so worried you'd leave me when you found out.' The laugh that came with her sentence sounded sour. 'Or that it'd change things between us.'

I hated the fact she'd doubted me enough to think we'd crumble because my sister knew about us. It humbled me.

'You know what's funny?' I asked, no humour in it. 'I left my parents' place so excited to see you and have an open and honest conversation about everything and tell you how I was falling for you.' I laughed sardonically. 'But then I had time here to myself and convinced myself you didn't feel the same way, and that you were taking a step back because you didn't want to be with me and didn't know how to tell me. I should've just asked you.' I shook my head, feeling like an idiot all over again. 'God, I'm sorry for making us both suffer.'

'I guess this is where we learn that open and honest communication is a two-way street that we both need to walk down more often.' Madison smiled, no anger or sadness living on her face.

I chuckled at that. 'Yeah, I'd say that's fair.'

'Okay, this is the part where we say something like: let's never be stupid again. Let's promise to always talk it out and tell each other when something's bothering us.'

'I can do that.' I squeezed her warm hand, still held in mine.

'Me too.'

'And while we're being honest,' I said, taking a deep breath. 'From the moment I bumped into you at Dottie's party, you mesmerised me. You are bewitching, Madison, and I never want to be parted from you.'

Yes, I quoted *Rules of Engagement*, that film all the girls adored. So sue me.

Madison, recognising the quote instantly, leaned forwards and hugged me, placing kisses on my neck, my cheeks, my lips.

'Wow, Dill. I thought you hated that movie,' she said when she stopped.

I manoeuvred us so my arm wrapped around her shoulders and she could lean into me the way I liked best.

'But you don't. Plus, Dahlia watches it a lot.'

'She does have a thing for the actor,' Madison said. 'If we're being honest, I have a thing for you.'

'You do? Coulda fooled me.'

She jabbed me in the ribs. 'Bull. I made it clear to you from Dot's party onwards about my feelings.'

I nodded, hoping my expression looked sombre. 'May as well have stuck a neon sign to your head.'

'One that read: I love you, Dylan Winters.'

Even though it was a joke, the phrase caught me off guard. My stomach flipped, a mix of anxiety and nerves and pure longing.

I'd blurted it out earlier, but she hadn't responded or acknowledged the declaration in any way.

A hush fell over the room.

Madison understood my hesitancy to break the moment, twisting in my arms so she could look into my eyes.

'I do, you know?' she said, blinking up at me with such innocence and love it would've knocked me back if I was standing.

'You do what?'

'Love you.' She placed a small kiss on my lips. 'I love you. And every day, I thank whatever is out there for everything that's happened between us.' She glanced at me, her look playful. 'Thank you for rejecting me.'

'I love you, too. And thank you for pushing me, even after I rejected you.'

Her eyes wrinkled at the corners from the force of her smile. 'Well, how else were you going to notice what was right in front of your face?'

madison

DYLAN WINTERS LOVED ME.

He loved me.

He actually loved me, for real, and not only in my dreams, or my wildest fantasies, or during the times I touched myself and thought of him.

Days had passed and I still couldn't believe it.

He hadn't left my side since, taking a couple of days off work to sit with me in the flat and watch films together like any couple. As if we didn't have a lot of crap to deal with outside of our happy bubble.

The bubble burst the moment Dylan went back to work, and I had to face the police and tell them everything that happened with Mum. It was the only way to have her arrested and charged and a restraining order put in place. They'd come to the hospital, but I wasn't sure yet whether I wanted to press charges. Talking to Bonnie and Dylan about it helped me make up my mind.

'How many times did Mrs James come to your house demanding money?'

The officer sitting across from me and Bonnie at the table looked stern, but looks could be deceiving. He was one of the nice ones. He'd helped me when I spent the night at the station reliving the murder, having to describe it again and again in as much detail as I could remember.

That night was a long one.

This conversation wasn't going much quicker.

'Three.'

'And how much did she say she owed?'

'Ten grand.'

'And did she tell you to whom she owed the money?'

I shook my head. 'She referred to them as bad people.'

The police asked more questions, and I answered them as best I could.

'Oh!' I said, a memory coming to me as the officer stood from his chair. He seated himself again and pulled out his pen and paper. 'She said a man named Ralph was meant to talk to me, or sort it, or something.' Her exact wording escaped me. 'A bald man watched my home the day before she first visited. I assume it was Ralph.'

The officer, whose name I'd promptly forgotten the moment he uttered it, looked at me with sorrow in his eyes. 'I'm sorry Miss Jones, but the Ralph in question was arrested and detained by us before the date you say your mum first visited. The man outside your flat wasn't Ralph.'

Panic rioted inside me. 'No?'

'No, Miss.'

'What about the note?' The note attached to Dylan's car the day we went to his parents for dinner. We never found out whether Mum sent it or not. 'Could that have been from my mum?'

'She says not, but there's no way to know for definite.' The officer's eyes watched me. 'We will get to the bottom of this.'

I nodded, my attention elsewhere.

Bonnie walked the officer out and returned to the dining room, a steaming cup of hot chocolate in her hand. 'Mike made this for you. Thought you might need it.'

'Thank you.' It had mini marshmallows and cream on top just the way I liked it. Tears filled my eyes at how much the two of them paid attention to me and my likes. 'Have I told you how much I love you?'

'You've mentioned it a couple of times, dear.' She placed the mug down in front of me. 'We love you more.'

Bonnie took the seat beside me. Her hand rubbed my arm, comforting me. I owed so much to the amazing woman next to me, it was hard to put it into words so she'd understand. She'd never let me down, not once. Stayed by my side in the hospital. Sat by my side while I told the police about everything.

Besides Dylan, she was my rock. My role model.

'Every single day, I thank my lucky stars that Dottie spoke to me at the playground,' I said, and I meant every word. Without Dottie and the rest of the Winters clan, I wouldn't be the same. Might not even exist at all.

The harrowing thought hurt.

'As am I.' Bonnie smiled, her front tooth stained slightly by her pale lipstick. 'Your mum won't hurt you again, Madison. Mike and I will make sure of it. Dylan, too, no doubt.'

'Thank you for being my other mother,' I whispered, trying to pour all my feelings into my gaze. I needed her to know how much it all meant to me.

'Madison, in every way, you are my daughter as much as my three girls. I am so glad you have Dylan and it's all sorted out the way it should. Just know, if for whatever reason, you and Dylan don't work out, I will always be here for you.'

My heart sang with happiness.

Just because my true parents never showed me love, it didn't mean I wasn't worthy of it.

Love came in many forms.

And I deserved each and every one.

dylan

THE MEETING STARTED AT TEN.

Everybody sat around the table, varying degrees of misery flickering in their expressions.

Jeoffrey and Mick were in a whispered conversation at the top of the table, each of them looking unimpressed with whatever they had to say.

My gut already knew.

'Okay, everyone,' Mick said as Jeoff took the last unoccupied seat. 'I know the rumours are swirling, so Jeoff and I thought it best to sit you all down and discuss it before things got out of hand.'

Noah, sitting opposite me, grimaced.

'As most of you know, there's a leak in the police department.' Mick's pacing made my head hurt, but at the same time, I couldn't tear my eyes away, watching him walk from left to right and back again. 'Right now, we've been asked to take a step back from the case until things make more sense.'

Whispers started up in the room.

'The higher-ups still want our help, and when they have

something to charge Lawrence or Jaws with, the case will go to trial.' Mick paused his pacing. 'Honestly, it's all a shitshow right now. As for the case against Malcolm Silver, he's pleaded guilty.'

The words washed over me. *Fuck.*

'Meaning there will be no trial, and Madison Jones won't have to give testimony.'

My heart soared. The fact the one I loved didn't have to stand up in court and repeat what she observed was a massive weight off my shoulders. Plus, it meant she wasn't drawing more potential attention from The Syndicate.

But also, it wasn't the outcome I wanted in regard to the case as a whole. Mixed emotions swirled in me.

We already knew the bald man outside her place wasn't the mysterious Ralph or anything to do with her mum. Could he be linked to The Syndicate? Only time would tell.

The note she received on the car also could've been from them, but then again, would her mum fess up if she had done it? Of course not.

Mick continued talking, but whatever he said, Noah could tell me later.

I got out my phone.

> Baby, got some good news to tell you later. Want to meet me for dinner? Could go to Carillo's? x

Her reply came instantaneously.

> Yes, please! Swear down their chicken burger is the best known to man. Dana sends her love x

The two of them were at some book fair in the city. Since we'd sorted everything out, Dana and Madison had spent more time together. We all knew Dana loved books, but it turned out that Mads also quite enjoyed them. She'd had to pass the time while in the hospital outside of Mum's visiting hours, and reading had taken the top spot.

> Does she want to join us? x

> She said no thanks. She's being super secretive … Maybe she's hiding Isaac's body x

> Don't even joke about it. I can't defend my sister in court if I know the details beforehand x

Mick coughed. 'Not keeping you from anything, are we, Dylan?'

I put my phone back into my pocket, not feeling anywhere near as sorry as I probably should.

'Sorry about that. Just passing along the good news to Madison.'

Mick's smirk said he knew more than I'd told him about my relationship status with Madison. My eyes went to Noah, who suspiciously looked away at that exact moment.

It was funny how quickly life could change.

If the case had fallen apart at the start of the year, I wouldn't have known how to cope.

Would've been lost without the constant drive of The Syndicate case nagging at me all hours of the day and night.

My work, my job, had made up so much of my time. So

much of my life. Yet now, that wasn't the case anymore. Madison, my girl—my life—meant more to me than work. And, damn, did that realisation feel good.

She was the thing that got me up in the morning and the last thought I had at night.

She made it all worth it.

And because of her, the loss of everything I'd worked towards only stung a little.

Because of her, I felt complete.

madison

'So I think it's time we have a talk, isn't it?'

Dylan's words were the equivalent of a bucket of ice-cold water being dumped on the top of my head, thoroughly soaking me, sending a chill through me.

They were the words he'd said before leaving me and putting us on a break. He didn't want to end things, did he?

'Excuse me?'

Three weeks had passed since I returned from hospital and Dylan came over to speak about everything. After that, we'd been attached at the hip, barely out of one another's sight for long.

We exchanged I love you.

He stayed over every night.

Yet we'd never actually defined our relationship since. Maybe he didn't think it was necessary. Who knew what went through that large brain of his?

And now he wanted to *talk*.

I tried not to let him witness my distress, but I guess I didn't do too good a job of it.

'Oh shit,' he said, pulling me into a hug. 'No, not like that! Sorry, poor wording.'

I laughed against his chest, the sound muffled. 'Poor is probably underplaying it.'

He chuckled. 'Okay, yeah, take the piss out of the doofus in the room.'

'You're not a doofus.' I stepped out of his embrace and looked up at his gorgeous face, getting lost in the dark pool of his eyes. 'You're just ... not always the brightest.'

'What a ringing endorsement.'

The two of us moved to the sofa and flopped down together, finding ourselves looking into one another's eyes.

'Hi.'

'Hi.'

'So, this talk ...' I said, ready for whatever he had to say.

'Ah, the talk.' He rubbed his jaw, freshly shaved. 'Right. Well. I was going to ask about your plans now that everything's over for you.'

'That's what you wanted to talk about?' I knocked his shoulder. 'You gave me a heart attack to ask me about my plans for the future?'

'Yeah, okay. We all know I messed up. Let's move on.'

'It's weird, posting again,' I said. Once Malcolm Silver pleaded guilty and I was no longer needed to give evidence, the police and the lawyers told me I could return to work. In the time I'd not posted, a lot of followers had left, understandably, and others had speculated about the real reason I'd fallen off the face of the earth. Also understandable. But it was never something I loved to do, and returning to it only made it feel more hollow than ever. 'I'm not sure I want to do it anymore. Or at least, not in the same way.'

Dylan moved a cushion and repositioned himself, his arm open wide for me to rest up against. I turned around so I could lie on my back and look up at him from below.

'What do you want to do in your heart?'

'My heart wants out of the inane influencing. For some people, it's the best kind of work. Like Dottie, for example. She loves it, and it fuels her in a way it never did for me.'

'Dottie loves the attention.'

'And that's her thing, and that's totally fine. But it's not *me*.'

'What would be?'

For some reason, fear stopped me from answering.

Dylan, who by now knew me as well as I knew myself, spoke the words for me.

'A YouTube commentary channel,' he said, certain, sure. 'That would be you all over.'

'You don't think it's a silly idea?'

'What? No!' He placed a gentle kiss on my forehead. 'I think you'd be perfect at it. People are always better at things if their heart is also attached.'

The rightness of it all startled me. As if the universe spoke to me personally, telling me it was the thing to do— the *only* thing to do.

Dylan continued, 'I'll support you in any way I can.'

'You will?'

'Duh!' We laughed, and the fact he'd mocked me didn't make me even a bit mad. 'And hey, why not do your first investigative video about something local?'

'Like the case of Malcolm Silver?' I asked, biting my bottom lip.

'Probably best not to antagonise The Syndicate more

than we already have, don't you think?' Dylan said with a chuckle. 'They're still out there, and they know who we are.' He paused, his face the one he made whenever he thought too hard. 'Hmm. Maybe there's a way to use it to our advantage.'

'We'll see.' I smiled at him. 'What about you? With the case stagnant for a bit, how are you gonna cope?'

'It'll be weird not working so hard, but I don't think I'll miss it. It gives us more time together.'

'How do you figure that?'

'Well, now you're not in the office every day, I don't get to spend as much time with you, and you're much more important than work.'

'I do miss the office.' I ran my fingers along his arm wrapped around my waist. 'Not getting to talk to Dawn every day is a bummer.'

Dylan pinched the small patch of skin available to him.

'I take it back. Of course it's you I miss seeing all the time.'

We fell into a comfortable silence.

After a few minutes, I had to break it. 'Dill?'

He hummed in answer.

'Are we *together*? Like a couple?'

'Of course we're a couple.' Dylan laughed, his chest vibrating beneath me. 'What did you think we were?'

'Oh, I don't know.' I chuckled at myself. 'I didn't want to assume anything.'

'You do make me laugh, babe.' He pushed me so I sat up and we could face one another. 'You're my girlfriend, and I'm your boyfriend. Does that clear it up?'

It sounded bloody odd, something so secondary school

coming from a thirty-year-old, but here we were, and it made me happy.

He leaned forwards, his long eyelashes fluttering as he moved closer to place a bruising but somehow still gentle kiss on my lips.

'It does.' I moved closer to him, not wanting a gap between us if the situation didn't call for it. 'And now we're one hundred per cent official,' I said with a wide smile. 'All we need to do is tell your family.'

'I'm sure they've already guessed.'

'Yes, but acting like a couple around them will be odd at first, don't you think?'

'Well, yeah ...'

'And it's your parents' anniversary party next weekend.'

'So it is.'

'Our first official outing as an *official* official couple.'

'How long do you think you'll use the word official?' he asked, the glint in his eye letting me know he was teasing.

'Oh, I don't know,' I said, pretending to think about it. 'Until you get bored of me, I suppose.'

'Well, lucky for you, that's never happening.'

dylan

EPILOGUE

MUM AND DAD'S TRANSFORMED GARDEN WAS filled with the people who loved them.

The two of them beamed at everybody who walked through the garden gate and thanked them for showing up. They were still so in love for a couple celebrating thirty years of marriage, and no, I wouldn't admit to it if you asked me, but it made me happy to know what true love was just from being in their presence.

My parents' best friends, Cara and Walter, a married couple who owned the café in town, were talking to Jimmy and Lola.

Noah and Hallie were hovering near Lola, most likely to keep an eye on her and make sure she didn't imbibe too many cocktails. Everybody knew Lola to be a live wire without alcohol, but with it? She became a real riot.

Even Dean had shown up, taking a break from his tour to fly back. He needed to be back on the plane later that day, but the fact he'd come meant a lot to our parents, and that was all that mattered.

My eyes were fixed on Madison on the other side of the garden, standing with Dana and Dottie, laughing at something Dana had said. Probably another scathing retort against her co-worker, Isaac.

'Damn, I missed a lot while I was gone,' Dean said, nudging his head in the girls' direction. 'Wanna give me the short version?'

I took a sip of my beer. The sun had made it warm—or maybe the way I gripped the glass in my hands had done that. 'Shortest version of all is that I'm in love with Madison Jones.'

'Yep, I'd say that qualifies as short.' Dean chuckled and took a sip from the can he nursed. 'Okay, how about the not-so-short but also not-so-long version?'

'Yes, Dylan. Do tell.' Noah had separated from Hallie and moved over to us. I spotted Hallie when I looked back to Madison, the two of them smiling and pointing over at us. I'd have to find out later what they were saying because clearly it involved me and Noah ...

'... Madison.'

Her name coming from Noah's lips pulled me back into the conversation. 'Sorry?'

'I was saying that it's rare now to get your attention away from Madison.' I couldn't find it in myself to get mad at Noah, even as a joke, because he spoke the truth.

'I go away for five months and come home to find you all loved up with Madison Jones, of all people. Lord knows what's gonna happen while I'm gone for the next few months.' We chuckled at the thought. Things moved rather fast around here. 'Did Dottie freak?'

'Dottie acted the way you're imagining Dottie acted.' I faked a shudder. 'She's working on it.'

'As long as you're happy, then so am I, bro. I think Mads will be good for you. Might make you stop working so hard, too.'

Noah chuckled at that. 'I've barely seen him at the office in the last month.'

'Bullshit. I—'

'Dylan Winters! Did you just swear in front of your younger brother?'

Mum appeared in front of us, stern eyes aimed my way, but a smile teasing at the edges of her mouth.

'Younger brother?' I scoffed. 'Dean's twenty-three and in a band! Pretty sure he hears a heck of a lot worse on a daily basis.'

'Doesn't mean you need to corrupt him further. Now, where is your sister? She messaged to say she was running a little late, but I expected her to be here by now. I can't keep Jimmy away from the buffet for much longer. He's practically wasting away!'

My eyes went to where Jimmy stood with Dad, and I had to refrain from laughing. I'd known him practically my whole life, and I could say with great certainty that the man had never wasted away a day in his life.

The girls' screaming drowned out Dean's no doubt cheeky response.

Noah and I shared a look and shrugged. Sometimes, ignoring the girls and their screeching made for a much easier life.

Dean, who hadn't learned the hard way yet, or had but

was determined to know the gossip regardless, called over to them. 'What's going on?'

'You will never guess what's just happened!' Dottie's jaw threatened to touch the grass. How did she open her mouth so wide?

Clearly, they wanted someone to either guess or ask to be put out of their misery.

I took one for the team when nobody else volunteered. 'What's happened?'

Madison answered, her eyes wide. 'Bridger Daniels has posted a picture of him and Dahlia! Together!' She took a deep breath. 'With the caption, *my one*!'

The girls squealed again, loud enough to burst the eardrums of anybody within a thirty-mile radius.

Noah nudged me. 'Bridger definitely hasn't mentioned anything of the sort.'

I said out of the side of my mouth, 'No, neither has Dahlia.'

Amidst the chaos, the garden gate opened to reveal a rather red-faced Dahlia, and standing a step behind her, an amused Bridger Daniels.

Everybody in the garden fell silent, their eyes transfixed on the couple at the gate.

Dahlia's gritted teeth smile told me all was not as it seemed. She may fool the others, but she'd never fool me.

'Sorry we're late, everyone. Guys, this is Bridger. Bridger, this is my family.'

To be continued...

Afterword

The story continues in *Lies of Love* with Dahlia and Bridger.

WANT MORE MADISON AND DYLAN WHILE YOU WAIT?

Scan the QR code below for an extended epilogue.

If you would like to join my newsletter to stay up to date with everything me, then scan the QR code below.

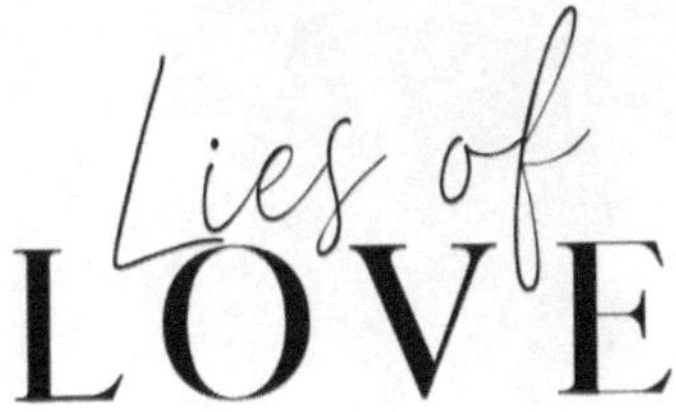

Book #2
Bridger & Dahlia
Trope: *Fake Relationship*

To continue reading, scan the QR code below
and head to *Lies of Love*:

Acknowledgements

Thank you to Megan, who is always there for me no matter the circumstances, and is a massive supporter of mine day in and day out.

Thank you to my baby cat Cress for being the cutest baby cat to ever exist—even if she does distract me from writing to whine for more food constantly.

Thank you to the fourway for always having my back, acting as a sounding board, and for just being all-around great girls. I am so thankful to you three for making the last four years better.

And a final thank you to you, readers. Without you, this journey would be mighty lonesome.

About K. Lowrie

Since a super young age, K. Lowrie has enjoyed reading and creating stories.

Book world is an escape and the best way to lose a day or two.

A list in no particular order of her greatest loves:
- Henry VIII and the Tudor era
- Her baby cat, Cress
- Musicals
- Disney
- Cheese

www.klowrieauthor.com

She loves to stalk people online (in a good way) and understands if you do too.

instagram.com/klowrieauthor

goodreads.com/klowrieauthor

facebook.com/klowrieauthor

bookbub.com/authors/k-lowrie

Also by K. Lowrie

Model Act

Model (mis)Behaviour

Acting Out

Lanes of Love

Law of Love

Lies of Love

www.ingramcontent.com/pod-product-compliance
Lightning Source LLC
Chambersburg PA
CBHW021218220726
48287CB00015B/1678